A TASTE OF
CHEKHOV

ANTON CHEKHOV

*An introduction to the works of the master storyteller,
via 9 stories spanning the last twenty years of his life.*

PAUL RICHARDSON

EDITOR

Translations: Paul Richardson: A Little Joke, The Dear Dog, Joy, Bliny. Lydia Razran-Stone and Constance Garnett: Man in a Case, Gooseberries, About Love. Paul Richardson and Constance Garnett: The Bride. Constance Garnett: Happiness.

ISBN 978-1-880100-05-9

StoryWorkz, Inc.
PO Box 567
Montpelier, VT 05601-0567
storyworkz.com

CONTENTS

"Man will only become better when we have
shown him to himself as he is."

– Anton Chekhov

JOY

It was twelve midnight.

Mitya Kuldarov, excited and dishevelled, flew into his parents' apartment, and hurriedly ran through all the rooms. His parents had already gone to bed. His sister lay in bed, reading the last page of a novel. His schoolboy brothers were asleep.

"Where have you been?" his parents cried in surprise. "What's the matter with you?

"Oh, don't ask! I never expected this! No, I never expected this! It's... it's simply unbelievable!"

Mitya laughed and sank into an armchair, unable to stand up, he was so happy.

"It's incredible! You can't even imagine! Look!"

His sister jumped out of bed, wrapped a quilt around her, and approached her brother. The schoolboys woke up.

"What's the matter? I hardly recognize you!"

"It's because I am overjoyed, Mama! Do you know, now all Russia knows of me! All of it! Until now, only you knew that there was a collegiate registrar[1] named Dmitry Kuldarov, and now all Russia knows it! Mama! Oh, Lord!"

Mitya jumped up, ran through all the rooms, and then sat down again.

"Why, what has happened? Speak plainly!"

"You live like wild animals, don't read the newspapers, and don't pay attention to publicity, yet there's so much excellent stuff in the papers. If anything happens it's known immediately, nothing is hidden! How happy I am! Oh, Lord! You know they only write about celebrated people in the papers, and now they have gone and written about me!"

"What do you mean? Where?"

Papa turned pale. Mama glanced at the holy image and crossed herself. The schoolboys jumped out of bed and, without dressing, approached their elder brother in their nightshirts.

"Yes-s! They have written about me! Now all Russia knows of me! Hang onto the paper, Mama, as a keepsake! We will read it from time to time! Look!"

Mitya pulled from his pocket the edition of the paper, gave it to his father, and pointed with his finger to a passage marked with blue pencil.

"Read!"

His father put on his glasses.

"Read it, already!"

Mama glanced at the holy image and crossed herself. Papa cleared his throat and began to read: "On the 29th of December, at eleven o'clock in the evening, collegiate registrar Dmitry Kuldarov..."

"You see, you see! Go on!"

"...collegiate registrar Dmitry Kuldarov, exiting the tavern in Kozikhin's building on Little Bronnaya, and in an intoxicated condition..."

---

1. Collegiate registrar – the lowest rank in the Russian Civil Service.

"That's me and Semyon Petrovich... It's described down to the last detail! Go on! Listen!"

"...in an intoxicated condition, slipped and fell beneath a horse standing there that belonged to the cabbie Ivan Drotov, a peasant of the village of Durykino, Yukhnovsky district. The frightened horse stepped over Kuldarov, drawing the sledge over him, which also contained Moscow merchant of the second guild Stepan Lukov, dashed down the street and was caught by some yardmen. Kuldarov, at first unconscious, was taken to the police station and there examined by a doctor. The blow which he received to the back of his head..."

"It was from the shaft, papa. Go on! Read the rest!"

"...he received on the back of his head was classified as not significant. A report was drawn up on the incident. The injured individual was given medical assistance."

"They applied a cold compress to the back of my head. You've read it then? Ah! So, you see. Now it's all over Russia! Give it here!"

Mitya seized the newspaper, folded it up and put it into his pocket.

"I'm going to run round to the Makarovs and show them... I must also show it to the Ivanitskys, and to Natasya Ivanovna, and Anisim Vasilyich... Gotta run! Goodbye!"

Mitya put on his cap with the cockade and, joyful and triumphant, ran outside.

1883

THE DEAR DOG

Lieutenant Dubov, a soldier in the army who was getting on in years, and the volunteer Knaps were sitting around enjoying a few drinks.

"An outstanding hound!" said Dubov, showing his dog Milka to Knaps. "Ex-cell-ent dog! Just take a look at her muzzle! A muzzle like that is priceless all by itself! You bump into a dog lover and he'd give you 200 rubles just for the muzzle! Don't believe me? Well, then you understand nothing at all…"

"I understand, but…"

"It's a Setter, a purebred English Setter! Such striking posture, and her sense of smell… shocking! Lord, such a nose! Do you know how much I paid for Milka, when she was still a pup? One hundred rubles! A remarkable dog! Scoun-drel, Milka! Id-i-ot, Milka! Come here, c'mere… you little dog, my doggie…"

Dubov pulled Milka in close and kissed her between the ears. Tears welled up in his eyes.

"I will not give you up to anyone… my beauty… you thief. Do you truly love me, Milka? Do you? Ah, get outta here," the lieutenant suddenly cried. "Putting your dirty paws all over my uniform! Yeah,

Knaps, I paid 150 rubles, for a pup! Surely it was worth it! My only regret: I've got no time to hunt! The dog is dying from boredom. Her talent is being wasted… So I have to sell her. Buy her, Knaps! You'll thank me the rest of your life. And, well, if you are short on money, then I will kindly halve the price… Take her for 50! It's a steal!"

"No, my dear fellow…" Knaps sighed. "If your Milka was a male, then I might have considered it, but…"

"Milka not a *male*?" the lieutenant replied, astonished. "Knaps, what is with you? Milka not… a male?! Ha-ha! Then what is she, in your opinion? A *bitch*? Ha-ha… Such a good little boy! He still can't tell the difference between a male and female hound!"

"You are talking to me as if I were blind or a baby…" Knaps said, taking offense. "Of course it is a bitch!"

"Perhaps you will then say that I am a lady?! Oh, Knaps, Knaps! You focus only on technical aspects. No, on my soul, this is an authentic, purebred male! And, what is more, it can beat any male hands down… but you… not a he! Ha-ha…"

"Excuse me, Mikhail Ivanovich, but you… you are simply treating me like a fool… It is rather insulting…"

"Well, no need, to hell with you… Don't buy her… No one is forcing you into it! Next thing you will be saying that this here is not her tail, but a leg… No need. I just wanted to do you a favor. Vakhrameyev, cognac!"

An orderly brought more cognac. The friends drank up another glass each and fell into thought. A half-hour of silence followed.

"And even if it were a female…" the lieutenant said, breaking the silence and staring bitterly at the bottle. "Surprise, surprise! It would be even better for you. She would give you puppies, and each one worth 25 rubles… They would all be snapped up. I don't know why you so insist on a male! Bitches are a thousand times better. Females are more grateful and affectionate… But, well, if you fear the female gender, well, kindly take it for 25."

"No, my dear fellow… I will not give you a kopek. First of all, I don't need a dog. And second, I don't have any money."

"You should have said so earlier. Milka, get outta here!"

The orderly brought out fried eggs. The friends set to them and silently cleaned out the frying pan.

"You're a good one, Knaps, you're honest," the lieutenant said, wiping his lips. "But it is sad for me to let you go this way… to hell with it, you know what? Take the dog for nothing!"

"What am I, dear fellow, to do with her?" Knaps said, sighing. "Who will walk her?"

"Ah, no need, no need… to hell with you! You don't want 'er, don't need 'er… Where're you off to? Sit down!"

Knaps, stretching himself, stood and put on his hat.

"Time to go, goodbye," he said, yawning.

"Hey, hold on, I'll walk you back."

Dubov and Knaps put on their coats and went outside. For a hundred steps or so, they walked in silence.

"You have any idea who I could give the dog to?" the lieutenant began. "Perhaps some acquaintance of yours? The dog, as you have seen, is very nice, pedigreed, but… well, I definitely don't need her!"

"Dunno, buddy… What sort of friends do I have here, really?"

Not another word was said until they reached Knaps' apartment. Only after Knaps shook the lieutenant's hand and opened his gate, did Dubov cough and blurt out, rather indecisively, "Do you know, do the local skinners take dogs or no?"

"They should take them… I really can't say."

"I'll go tomorrow with Vakhrameyev… To hell with her, let them take her hide… Nasty dog! Repulsive! It's not enough that she messes up my rooms, but yesterday she went into the kitchen and ate up all the meat, v-v-vile creature… All fine and well if it had a good pedigree, but the devil knows what it is – probably a mix of a mongrel and a pig. G'night!"

"G'bye," Knaps said.

The gate slammed shut and the lieutenant stood alone in the street.

1885

A LITTLE JOKE

It is noon on a clear winter's day. There is a strong, ringing frost, and Nadenka, who is clutching my arm, is dusted with a silvery hoarfrost on the curls at her temples and the down of her upper lip. We are standing on a tall hill. A sledding hill stretches from our feet to the field below, the sun reflecting off it like a mirror. All about us are little sleds, covered in bright, red woolen cloths.

"Let's ride down, Nadezhda Petrovna!" I beg. "Just once! I promise you we'll arrive safe and unharmed."

But Nadenka is afraid. The expanse between her little galoshes and the bottom of the icy hill is to her a strange, immeasurably deep abyss. Her spirit falters and her breath catches when she looks down the hill, when I propose that we ride the sleds. What might happen if she dared to launch into the abyss!? She might die, or go insane.

"I beg you!" I say. "There is nothing to fear! It's just faint-heartedness, cowardice!"

Finally Nadenka relents and I can see that she has done so despite the fact that she fears for her life. I sit her down, pale and trembling, on the sled, wrapping my arms around her, and together we hurtle into the chasm.

The sled flies like a bullet. The cloven air strikes our faces, roaring and whistling past our ears, it tears and burns painfully, furiously, as if it wants to rip our heads from our shoulders. The pressure of the wind makes breathing impossible. It feels like the devil himself has seized us in his clutches and, with a roar, is pulling us into hell. Everything around us blurs into a single, long, impetuously rushing streak… Just one moment more and we will surely die!

"I love you, Nadya!" I say in a low voice.

Bit by bit, the sled begins to slow. The roar of the wind and the buzz of the runners is no longer so frightening. Our breathing returns to normal and finally we are at the bottom. Nadenka is neither dead nor alive. She is completely pale, barely breathing… I help her to stand up.

"I would not do that again for anything," she says, looking at me with wide, horror-filled eyes. "Not for anything in the world! I almost died!"

A little bit later, she recovers and starts to peer probingly into my eyes: did I say those four words, or did she merely imagine them in the rush of the whirlwind? But I stand near her, smoking, closely examining my gloves.

She takes my arm and we stroll for a long time around the hills. The mystery, apparently, unnerves her. Were those words voiced or not? Yes or no? Yes or no? It is a question of pride, honor, life, happiness, a very important question, the most important one in the world. Nadenka impatiently, sadly, looks at me with a penetrating glare, replies absentmindedly, waits to see if I will speak. Oh, such a performance by this tender face, such a performance! I can see that she is struggling with herself, she needs to say something, to ask something, but she cannot find the words, she is awkward, afraid, unable to be happy.

"You know what?" she says, not looking at me.

"What?" I ask.

"Let's… ride one more time."

We climb the stairs up the hill. Again I set a pale, trembling Nadenka onto the sled, again we fly into the awful abyss, again the wind roars and the runners buzz, and again at the most powerful and loudest point of the ride I say in a low voice:

"I love you, Nadenka!"

When the sled comes to a stop, Nadenka casts her glance at the hill we just rode down, then looks into my face for a long time, listening to my indifferent and impassive voice, and every inch of her – even her muff and hood – her entire body expresses extreme bewilderment. And it is written on her face: "What is going on? Who spoke those words? Him, or did I only imagine them?"

This uncertainty unnerves her, exasperates her. The poor girl does not respond to questions, glowers, is on the verge of crying.

"Shall we head home?" I ask.

"I um… like this sledding," she says, blushing. "Can we go again?"

She "likes" this sledding, and yet, sitting on the sled, just as before, she is pale, barely breathing from fear, trembling.

We descend a third time, and I notice that she is staring at my face, watching my lips. But I put a handkerchief to my lips, cough, and, when we are midway down the hill, successfully utter:

"I love you, Nadya!"

And the mystery holds! Nadenka is silent, thinking about something… I accompany her home from the park, she tries to go quietly, slowing her steps and waiting, to see if I will say those words to her. I can see how her soul is suffering, how she is forcing herself not to say, "It cannot be that the wind spoke those words! I don't want it to be the wind that spoke!"

The morning of the next day I receive a note: "If you are going sledding today, then come by and get me. N." And from that day forward, Nadenka and I start going sledding every day. And every time we fly down the hill on the sleds, I pronounce in a low voice the same words:

"I love you, Nadya!"

Nadenka quickly becomes accustomed to this phrase, as if to wine or morphine. She cannot live without it. Sure, flying down the hill is as scary as before, but now the fear and danger impart a special charm to these words of love, words which as before compose a mystery and torture the soul. There are still the same two suspects: the wind and I... Which of these two is declaring its love for her, she knows not, but apparently it is all the same to her; it doesn't matter what glass you drink from, as long as you get drunk.

Once, about midday, I went sledding alone; blending in with the crowd, I watch Nadenka approach the hill, her eyes searching for me... Then she timidly climbed the stairs... It is scary to ride alone, oh, so scary! She is pale as snow, trembling, going as if to her execution, but she goes, she goes decisively, recklessly. Apparently, she has decided to finally test it: will she hear those marvelously sweet words when I am not there? I see her sit on the sled, pale, her mouth clenched from fear. She closes her eyes and bids farewell to this world, inching forward... "Buzzzz" ring the runners. I don't know if Nadenka will hear those words. I only see her get up from the sled exhausted, weak. And I can tell from the look on her face that she does not know if she heard anything or not. The fear, as she sped down the hill, stole her ability to hear, to distinguish sounds, to understand...

And then spring – the month of March – arrives... the sun becomes gentler. Our icy hill warms, loses its luster and finally melts. We stop going sledding. Poor Nadenka no longer hears those words, there is no one to pronounce them, since the wind is silent and I am heading to Petersburg for a long time, perhaps for good.

About two days before my departure, I sit in the garden at dusk. A high wooden fence separates this garden from the courtyard where Nadenka lives... It is still rather cold, there is still snow under the manure. The trees are lifeless, but the air already smells of spring and the rooks are cawing noisily, sorting themselves out in their evening roost. I approach the fence and stare for a long while through a crack. I watch Nadenka come out onto the porch and fix a sad, longing gaze toward the sky… The spring breeze blows straight into her pale, mournful face… It reminds her of the wind that once tore into us on that hill, when she heard those four words, and her face becomes sad, so sad. A tear rolls down her face… And the poor girl stretches out both her arms, as if to ask the wind to once more deliver those words. And I, timing it to the wind, say in a low voice:

"I love you, Nadya!"

My Lord, how Nadya reacts! She cries out, her whole face smiles, and she reaches her arms out to embrace the wind. She is so joyful, so happy, so beautiful.

And I go inside to pack…

This was long ago. Nadenka is now married – either it was arranged, or she herself arranged it, no matter – to a departmental secretary for stewarding noble affairs, and has three children. That we once sledded together and that wind carried the words to her "I love you, Nadenka," is not forgotten; this is for her the happiest, most moving, and wonderful memory of her life…

As to me, now that I am older, I can no longer recall why I said those words, why I played that little joke…

1886

BLINY

Did you know that *bliny* have been around for over a thousand years, since what is known as the old Slavonic *ab ovo*...? They appeared on arth before Russian history began and have lived through it all, from the beginning to the last page, without any doubt, invented, like the samovar, by Russian minds... In anthropology, they should have as honored a place as twenty-foot ferns and stone knives; if we still haven't had any scientific research done on *bliny*, then that can only be because eating *bliny* is much easier than racking your brains over them...

Times change and ancient customs, dress and songs are gradually disappearing in Russia; much has gone already, and is only interesting historically, but meanwhile such triviality as *bliny* occupies the same firm and established place in the repertoire of today's Russia as it did 1,000 years ago. Nor is their end in sight...

Bearing in mind the respected age of *bliny* and their extraordinary steadfastness, certified by the centuries, in the struggle against innovation, it is sad to think that these tasty lumps of batter serve only narrow culinary and gastronomic purposes... Sad because of their antiquity, and their exemplary and purely Spartan steadfastness... Law, cuisine and stomachs do not last a thousand years.

As for me, I'm almost certain that these most eloquent elder statesmen have other ultimate purposes than the culinary and gastronomic... Besides the heavy and barely digestible batter, there is something more lofty, symbolic, even perhaps prophetic concealed in them... But what exactly?

I don't know, and I will never know. It constituted and constitutes hitherto... a deep, impenetrable *womanly secret*, about as difficult to crack as it is to force a bear to laugh... Yes, *bliny*, their meaning and destiny are the secret of wom n, one which men are not likely to find out soon. That's a good subject for an operetta.

Since prehistoric times, the Russian woman has religiously kept this secret, passing it down from generation to generation, exclusively from mother to daughter and granddaughter. If, God forbid, just one man were to find it out, then something would happen so terrible that even women couldn't imagine. Neither wife, nor sister, nor daughter... no woman will give away this secret to you, however dear you are to her, however far she has fallen. This is not a secret to be bought or bartered. No woman will utter it, not in the heat of passion, not in delirium. In a word, this is the only secret which has, over the course of 1,000 years, been able to avoid leaking through that fine sieve which is the fairer sex!

How are *bliny* baked? This is not known... Only the distant future will find out, we, meanwhile, should not analyze or ask questions, but just eat what we are given... It's a secret!

You will say that men make *bliny* too... Yes, but men's *bliny* are not *bliny*. A cold wind issues from their nostrils, they have the texture of rubber galoshes and their taste is far inferior to women's... Male cooks should withdraw and admit defeat...

Making *bliny* is an exclusively female affair... It is high time that male cooks realized that it's not just a process of pouring batter into hot frying pans, but a solemn rite, a whole complex system encompassing beliefs, traditions, language, prejudices, joys and suffering... Yes, suffering... If [Nikolai] Nekrasov said that the Russian woman is worn out by suffering, then it is *bliny* which are partly to blame...

I don't know what the process of making *bliny* consists of, but I have some notion of the mysteriousness and ceremony with which woman has surrounded this ritual... There is much mysticism, fantasy and even spiritualism involved... If you watch a woman making *bliny*, you may get the impression that she is summoning up spirits or extracting a philosophical stone from the batter.

First of all, no woman, however enlightened, would under any circumstances start making *bliny* on the 13th or on the eve of the 13th, or on Sunday evening or Monday. At these times *bliny* don't turn out well. Many shrewd women get round this by starting their baking long before *maslenitsa*, so that the household has the chance to eat *bliny* on *maslenitsa* Monday and on the 13th.

Second, the evening before making the *bliny*, the mistress of the house always whispers something secretly to the cook. They whisper and look at each other with eyes like they were composing a love letter... After the whispering, they usually send Yegorka the kitchen boy to the shop to buy yeast... The housekeeper then stares for a long time at the yeast, sniffs it, and however ideal it is, will undoubtedly say:

"This yeast is no good. Go and tell them to give you some better stuff, you wretched boy..."

The boy runs off and brings some new yeast... Then a large clay jar will be fetched and filled with water, and the yeast dissolved in it with a little flour... When the yeast is in, the mistress of the house and the cook go pale, cover the jar with an old cloth and put it in a warm place.

"Make sure you don't oversleep, Matryona..." whispers the mistress. "And keep the jar in a warm place at all times!"

There follows an anxious and wearisome night. Both the housekeeper and the cook suffer from insomnia, and if they sleep, then they are delirious and have terrible dreams... How lucky you men are that you don't make *bliny*!

Before the gloomy morning starts to lighten, the mistress of the house, barefoot, straggly haired, and dressed in just a nightshirt, runs down to the kitchen.

"Well? How is everything?" she says, hurling her questions at Matryona. "Answer me then!"

Matryona, meanwhile, is standing by the jar and pouring buckwheat flour into it...

Third, the women watch closely to make sure that no male, whether from the household or an outsider, enters the kitchen while *bliny* are being made... Cooks will not even let firemen in at this time. No one is allowed to enter, have a look or ask any questions... If anyone should look into the clay jar and say: "What excellent batter!" then you may as well pour it away because the *bliny* won't be a success! What women say or what spells they read during the making of *bliny*, no one knows.

Exactly half an hour before the batter is poured into the frying pan, the red-faced and by now exhausted cook pours a little hot water or warm milk into the jar. The mistress stands beside her. She wants to say something, but under the influence of holy terror is unable to speak. The other members of the household, meanwhile, pace around the rooms in expectation and, looking into the face of the housekeeper as she keeps rushing into the kitchen, get the feelings that there is someone giving birth there, or, at the least, getting married.

Then, at last, the first frying pan hisses, then a second, a third... The first three *bliny* are defective – Yegorka can eat those... but the fourth, fifth, sixth etc. go onto the plate, are covered with a napkin and carried into the dining room to the craving diners. The woman of the house, red-faced, beaming, and proud, brings the *bliny* herself... Anyone would think she had in her arms not *bliny*, but her firstborn.

So how is this triumphant sight to be explained? By evening, the lady and the cook are too tired to either stand or sit. They truly look as if they are suffering... A little more, it seems, and they'll give up the ghost.

That's the superficialities of the sacred rite. If the *bliny* were meant exclusively for the ignoble satisfaction of the stomach, then let's face it, neither the mysteriousness, nor the nighttime activities, nor the suffering would be comprehensible... Obviously there is something there, and this "something" is carefully hidden.

When you look at the ladies, you can certainly draw the conclusion that, in the future, *bliny* are going to carry out some great mission of world importance.

1886

HAPPINESS

A flock of sheep was spending the night on the broad steppe road that is called the great highway. Two shepherds were guarding it. One, a toothless old man of eighty, with a tremulous face, was lying on his stomach at the very edge of the road, leaning his elbows on the dusty leaves of a plantain; the other, a young fellow with thick black eyebrows and no moustache, dressed in the coarse canvas of which cheap sacks are made, was lying on his back, with his arms under his head, looking upwards at the sky, where the stars were slumbering and the Milky Way lay stretched exactly above his face.

The shepherds were not alone. A couple of yards from them in the dusk that shrouded the road a horse made a patch of darkness, and, beside it, leaning against the saddle, stood a man in high boots and a short full-skirted jacket who looked like an overseer on some big estate. Judging from his upright and motionless figure, from his manners, and his behavior to the shepherds and to his horse, he was a serious, reasonable man who knew his own value; even in the darkness signs could be detected in him of military carriage and of the majestically condescending expression gained by frequent intercourse with the gentry and their stewards.

The sheep were asleep. Against the grey background of the dawn, already beginning to cover the eastern part of the sky, the silhouettes of sheep that were not asleep could be seen here and there; they stood with drooping heads, thinking. Their thoughts, tedious and oppressive, called forth by images of nothing but the broad steppe and the sky, the days and the nights, probably weighed upon them themselves, crushing them into apathy; and, standing there as though rooted to the earth, they noticed neither the presence of a stranger nor the uneasiness of the dogs.

The drowsy, stagnant air was full of the monotonous noise inseparable from a summer night on the steppes; the grasshoppers chirruped incessantly; the quails called, and the young nightingales trilled languidly half a mile away in a ravine where a stream flowed and willows grew.

The overseer had halted to ask the shepherds for a light for his pipe. He lighted it in silence and smoked the whole pipe; then, still without uttering a word, stood with his elbow on the saddle, plunged in thought. The young shepherd took no notice of him, he still lay gazing at the sky while the old man slowly looked the overseer up and down and then asked:

"Why, aren't you Panteley from Makarov's estate?"

"That's myself," answered the overseer.

"To be sure, I see it is. I didn't know you – that is a sign you will be rich. Where has God brought you from?"

"From the Kovylyevsky fields."

"That's a good way. Are you letting the land on the part-crop system?"

"Part of it. Some like that, and some we are letting on lease, and some for raising melons and cucumbers. I have just come from the mill."

A big shaggy old sheepdog of a dirty white color with woolly tufts about its nose and eyes walked three times quietly round the horse, trying to seem unconcerned in the presence of strangers, then all at once dashed suddenly from behind at the overseer with an angry aged growl; the other dogs could not refrain from leaping up too.

"Lie down, you damned brute," cried the old man, raising himself on his elbow; "blast you, you devil's creature."

When the dogs were quiet again, the old man resumed his former attitude and said quietly:

"It was at Kovyli on Ascension Day that Yefim Zhmenya died. Don't speak of it in the dark, it is a sin to mention such people. He was a wicked old man. I dare say you have heard."

"No, I haven't."

"Yefim Zhmenya, the uncle of Styopka, the blacksmith. The whole district round knew him. Aye, he was a cursed old man, he was! I knew him for sixty years, ever since Tsar Alexander who beat the French was brought from Taganrog to Moscow.[1] We went together to meet the dead Tsar, and in those days the great highway did not run to Bahmut, but from Esaulovka to Gorodishche, and where Kovyli is now, there were bustards' nests – there was a bustard's nest at every step. Even then I had noticed that Yefim had given his soul to damnation, and that the Evil One was in him. I have observed that if any man of the peasant class is apt to be silent, takes up with old women's jobs, and tries to live in solitude, there is no good in it, and Yefim from his youth up was always one to hold his tongue and look at you sideways, he always seemed to be sulky and bristling like a cock before a hen. To go to church or to the tavern or to lark in the street with the lads was not his fashion, he would rather sit alone or be whispering with old women. When he was still young he took jobs to look after the bees and the market gardens. Good folks would come to his market garden

---

1. Alexander I, who defeated Napoleon, died December 1, 1825, while visiting Taganrog. Confusion and desire for reform surrounding his succession led to the Decembrist uprising.

sometimes and his melons were whistling. One day he caught a pike, when folks were looking on, and it laughed aloud, 'Ho-ho-ho-ho!'"

"It does happen," said Panteley.

The young shepherd turned on his side and, lifting his black eyebrows, stared intently at the old man.

"Did you hear the melons whistling?" he asked.

"Hear them I didn't, the Lord spared me," sighed the old man, "but folks told me so. It is no great wonder... the Evil One will begin whistling in a stone if he wants to. Before the Day of Freedom[2] a rock was humming for three days and three nights in our parts. I heard it myself. The pike laughed because Yefim caught a devil instead of a pike."

The old man remembered something. He got up quickly on to his knees and, shrinking as though from the cold, nervously thrusting his hands into his sleeves, he muttered in a rapid womanish gabble:

"Lord save us and have mercy upon us! I was walking along the river bank one day to Novopavlovka. A storm was gathering, such a tempest it was, preserve us Holy Mother, Queen of Heaven.... I was hurrying on as best I could, I looked, and beside the path between the thorn bushes – the thorn was in flower at the time – there was a white bullock coming along. I wondered whose bullock it was, and what the devil had sent it there for. It was coming along and swinging its tail and moo-oo-oo! but would you believe it, friends, I overtake it, I come up close – and it's not a bullock, but Yefim – holy, holy, holy! I make the sign of the cross while he stares at me and mutters, showing the whites of his eyes; wasn't I frightened! We came alongside, I was afraid to say a word to him – the thunder was crashing, the sky was streaked with lightning, the willows were bent right down to the water – all at once, my friends, God strike me dead that I die impenitent, a hare ran across the path... it ran and stopped, and said like a man: 'Good-evening,

---

2. Tsar Alexander II's emancipation of the serfs, announced in 1856 and which came into force February 19, 1861 (March 3, New Style).

peasants.' Lie down, you brute!" the old man cried to the shaggy dog, who was moving round the horse again. "Plague take you!"

"It does happen," said the overseer, still leaning on the saddle and not stirring; he said this in the hollow, toneless voice in which men speak when they are plunged in thought.

"It does happen," he repeated, in a tone of profundity and conviction.

"Ugh, he was a nasty old fellow," the old shepherd went on with somewhat less fervor. "Five years after the Freedom he was flogged by the commune at the office, so to show his spite he took and sent the throat illness upon all Kovyli. Folks died out of number, lots and lots of them, just as in cholera..."

"How did he send the illness?" asked the young shepherd after a brief silence.

"We all know how, there is no great cleverness needed where there is a will to it. Yefim murdered people with viper's fat. That is such a poison that folks will die from the mere smell of it, let alone the fat."

"That's true," Panteley agreed.

"The lads wanted to kill him at the time, but the old people would not let them. It would never have done to kill him; he knew the place where the treasure is hidden, and not another soul did know. The treasures about here are charmed so that you may find them and not see them, but he did see them. At times he would walk along the river bank or in the forest, and under the bushes and under the rocks there would be little flames, little flames... little flames as though from brimstone. I have seen them myself. Everyone expected that Yefim would show people the places or dig the treasure up himself, but he – as the saying is, like a dog in the manger – so he died without digging it up himself or showing other people."

The overseer lit a pipe, and for an instant illuminated his big moustaches and his sharp, stern-looking, and dignified nose. Little circles of light danced from his hands to his cap, raced over the saddle along the horse's back, and vanished in its mane near its ears.

"There are lots of hidden treasures in these parts," he said.

And slowly stretching, he looked round him, resting his eyes on the whitening east and added:

"There must be treasures."

"To be sure," sighed the old man, "one can see from every sign there are treasures, only there is no one to dig them, brother. No one knows the real places; besides, nowadays, you must remember, all the treasures are under a charm. To find them and see them you must have a talisman, and without a talisman you can do nothing, lad. Yefim had talismans, but there was no getting anything out of him, the bald devil. He kept them, so that no one could get them."

The young shepherd crept two paces nearer to the old man and, propping his head on his fists, fastened his fixed stare upon him. A childish expression of terror and curiosity gleamed in his dark eyes, and seemed in the twilight to stretch and flatten out the large features of his coarse young face. He was listening intently.

"It is even written in the Scriptures that there are lots of treasures hidden here," the old man went on, "it is so for sure... and no mistake about it. An old soldier of Novopavlovka was shown at Ivanovka a writing, and in this writing it was printed about the place of the treasure and even how many pounds of gold was in it and the sort of vessel it was in; they would have found the treasures long ago by that writing, only the treasure is under a spell, you can't get at it."

"Why can't you get at it, grandfather?" asked the young man.

"I suppose there is some reason, the soldier didn't say. It is under a spell... you need a talisman."

The old man spoke with warmth, as though he were pouring out his soul before the overseer. He talked through his nose and, being unaccustomed to talking much and rapidly, stuttered; and, conscious of his defects, he tried to adorn his speech with gesticulations of the hands and head and thin shoulders, and at every movement his hempen shirt crumpled into folds, slipped upwards and displayed his back, black with age and sunburn. He kept pulling it down, but it slipped up again at once. At last, as though driven out of all patience by the rebellious shirt, the old man leaped up and said bitterly:

"There is fortune, but what is the good of it if it is buried in the earth? It is just riches wasted with no profit to anyone, like chaff or sheep's dung, and yet there are riches there, lad, fortune enough for all the country round, but not a soul sees it! It will come to this, that the gentry will dig it up or the government will take it away. The gentry have begun digging the barrows... They scented something! They are envious of the peasants' luck! The government, too, is looking after itself. It is written in the law that if any peasant finds the treasure he is to take it to the authorities! I dare say, wait till you get it! There is a brew but not for you!"

The old man laughed contemptuously and sat down on the ground. The overseer listened with attention and agreed, but from his silence and the expression of his figure it was evident that what the old man told him was not new to him, that he had thought it all over long ago, and knew much more than was known to the old shepherd.

"In my day, I must own, I did seek for fortune a dozen times," said the old man, scratching himself nervously. "I looked in the right places, but I must have come on treasures under a charm. My father looked for it, too, and my brother, too – but not a thing did they find, so they died without luck. A monk revealed to my brother Ilya – the Kingdom of Heaven be his – that in one place in the fortress of Taganrog there was a treasure under three stones, and that that treasure was under a charm, and in those days – it was, I remember, in the year '38 – an Armenian used to live at Matveyev Barrow who sold talismans. Ilya bought a talisman, took two other fellows with him, and went to Taganrog. Only when he got to the place in the fortress, brother, there was a soldier with a gun, standing at the very spot..."

A sound suddenly broke on the still air, and floated in all directions over the steppe. Something in the distance gave a menacing bang, crashed against stone, and raced over the steppe, uttering, "Tah! tah! tah! tah!" When the sound had died away the old man looked inquiringly at Panteley, who stood motionless and unconcerned.

"It's a bucket broken away at the pits," said the young shepherd after a moment's thought.

It was by now getting light. The Milky Way had turned pale and gradually melted like snow, losing its outlines; the sky was becoming dull and dingy so that you could not make out whether it was clear or covered thickly with clouds, and only from the bright leaden streak in the East and from the stars that lingered here and there could one tell what was coming.

The first noiseless breeze of morning, cautiously stirring the spurges and the brown stalks of last year's grass, fluttered along the road.

The overseer roused himself from his thoughts and tossed his head. With both hands he shook the saddle, touched the girth and, as though he could not make up his mind to mount the horse, stood still again, hesitating.

"Yes," he said, "your elbow is near, but you can't bite it. There is fortune, but there is not the wit to find it."

And he turned facing the shepherds. His stern face looked sad and mocking, as though he were a disappointed man.

"Yes, so one dies without knowing what happiness is like…" he said emphatically, lifting his left leg into the stirrup. "A younger man may live to see it, but it is time for us to lay aside all thought of it."

Stroking his long moustaches covered with dew, he seated himself heavily on the horse and screwed up his eyes, looking into the distance, as though he had forgotten something or left something unsaid. In the bluish distance, where the furthest visible hillock melted into the mist, nothing was stirring; the ancient barrows, once watch-mounds and tombs, which rose here and there above the horizon and the boundless steppe had a sullen and death-like look; there was a feeling of endless time and utter indifference to man in their immobility and silence;

another thousand years would pass, myriads of men would die, while they would still stand as they had stood, with no regret for the dead nor interest in the living, and no soul would ever know why they stood there, and what secret of the steppes was hidden under them.

The rooks awakening, flew one after another in silence over the earth. No meaning was to be seen in the languid flight of those long-lived birds, nor in the morning which is repeated punctually every twenty-four hours, nor in the boundless expanse of the steppe.

The overseer smiled and said:

"What space, Lord have mercy upon us! You would have a hunt to find treasure in it! Here," he went on, dropping his voice and making a serious face, "here there are two treasures buried for a certainty. The gentry don't know of them, but the old peasants, particularly the soldiers, know all about them. Here, somewhere on that ridge (the overseer pointed with his whip) robbers one time attacked a caravan of gold; the gold was being taken from Petersburg to the Emperor Peter, who was building a fleet at the time at Voronezh. The robbers killed the men with the caravan and buried the gold, but did not find it again afterwards. Another treasure was buried by our Cossacks of the Don. In the year '12 they carried off lots of plunder of all sorts from the French, goods and gold and silver. When they were going homewards they heard on the way that the government wanted to take away all the gold and silver from them. Rather than give up their plunder like that to the government for nothing, the brave fellows took and buried it, so that their children, anyway, might get it; but where they buried it no one knows."

"I have heard of those treasures," the old man muttered grimly.

"Yes..." Panteley pondered again. "So it is..."

A silence followed. The overseer looked dreamily into the distance, gave a laugh and pulled the rein, still with the same expression as though he had forgotten something or left something unsaid. The horse reluctantly started at a walking pace. After riding a hundred paces

Panteley shook his head resolutely, roused himself from his thoughts and, lashing his horse, set off at a trot.

The shepherds were left alone.

"That was Panteley from Makarov's estate," said the old man. "He gets a hundred and fifty a year and provisions fund, too. He is a man of education..."

The sheep, waking up – there were about three thousand of them – began without zest to while away the time, nipping at the low, half-trampled grass. The sun had not yet risen, but by now all the barrows could be seen and, like a cloud in the distance, Saur's Grave with its peaked top.[3] If one clambered up on that tomb one could see the plain from it, level and boundless as the sky, one could see villages, manor houses, the settlements of the Germans and of the Molokani, and a long-sighted Kalmuck could even see the town and the railway station. Only from there could one see that there was something else in the world besides the silent steppe and the ancient barrows, that there was another life that had nothing to do with buried treasure and the thoughts of sheep.

The old man felt beside him for his crook – a long stick with a hook at the upper end – and got up. He was silent and thoughtful. The young shepherd's face had not lost the look of childish terror and curiosity. He was still under the influence of what he had heard in the night, and impatiently awaiting fresh stories.

"Grandfather," he asked, getting up and taking his crook, "what did your brother Ilya do with the soldier?"

The old man did not hear the question. He looked absent-mindedly at the young man, and answered, mumbling with his lips:

---

3. A burial mound in Donetsk region, due north of Taganrog. It was the site of an important World War II battle and held a memorial until 2014, when it was demolished amid fighting in Eastern Ukraine.

"I keep thinking, Sanka, about that writing that was shown to that soldier at Ivanovka. I didn't tell Panteley – God be with him – but you know in that writing the place was marked out so that even a woman could find it. Do you know where it is? At Bogata Bylochka at the spot, you know, where the ravine parts like a goose's foot into three little ravines; it is the middle one."

"Well, will you dig?"

"I will try my luck... "

"And, grandfather, what will you do with the treasure when you find it?"

"Do with it?" laughed the old man. "H'm!... If only I could find it then... I would show them all... H'm!... I should know what to do..."

And the old man could not answer what he would do with the treasure if he found it. That question had presented itself to him that morning probably for the first time in his life, and judging from the expression of his face, indifferent and uncritical, it did not seem to him important and deserving of consideration. In Sanka's brain another puzzled question was stirring: why was it only old men searched for hidden treasure, and what was the use of earthly happiness to people who might die any day of old age? But Sanka could not put this perplexity into words, and the old man could scarcely have found an answer to it.

An immense crimson sun came into view surrounded by a faint haze. Broad streaks of light, still cold, bathing in the dewy grass, lengthening out with a joyous air as though to prove they were not weary of their task, began spreading over the earth. The silvery wormwood, the blue flowers of the pig's onion, the yellow mustard, the cornflowers – all burst into gay colors, taking the sunlight for their own smile.

The old shepherd and Sanka parted and stood at the further sides of the flock. Both stood like posts, without moving, staring at the ground and thinking. The former was haunted by thoughts of fortune, the latter was pondering on what had been said in the night; what interested him was not the fortune itself, which he did not want and could not imagine, but the fantastic, fairy-tale character of human happiness.

A hundred sheep started and, in some inexplicable panic as at a signal, dashed away from the flock; and as though the thoughts of the sheep – tedious and oppressive – had for a moment infected Sanka also, he, too, dashed aside in the same inexplicable animal panic, but at once he recovered himself and shouted:

"You crazy creatures! You've gone mad, plague take you!"

When the sun, promising long hours of overwhelming heat, began to bake the earth, all living things that in the night had moved and uttered sounds were sunk in drowsiness. The old shepherd and Sanka stood with their crooks on opposite sides of the flock, stood without stirring, like fakirs at their prayers, absorbed in thought. They did not heed each other; each of them was living in his own life. The sheep were pondering, too.

1887

THE MAN IN A CASE

Some hunters, out too late to return home, were spending the night on the outskirts of Mironositskoye village in a barn belonging to Prokofy, the village elder. There were two of them, Ivan Ivanich, a veterinarian, and Burkin, a schoolmaster. Ivan Ivanich had a rather strange, double-barrelled surname – Chimsha-Gimalaysky – which did not suit him at all, and so he was called simply Ivan Ivanich all over the province. He lived on the stud farm near town and had come out shooting as a means of getting some fresh air. Burkin, who taught at the high school in town, would come to visit Count P. every summer, and had been thoroughly at home in this district for years.

They did not go to sleep immediately. Ivan Ivanich, a tall, lean old fellow with a long moustache, was sitting outside the door, smoking a pipe in the moonlight. Burkin was lying inside on the hay, invisible in the darkness.

They got to telling stories. Among other things, they spoke of the fact that the elder's wife, Mavra, a healthy and by no means stupid woman, had never been beyond her native village. She had never seen a large town or a railway in her life and had spent the last ten years sitting close to the stove, only venturing outside at night.

"What so surprising about that?" said Burkin. "There are plenty of people in the world who are solitary in temperament and, like hermit crabs or snails, try to retreat into their shells. Perhaps this is a kind of atavism, a return to the period when man's ancestors were not yet social animals and lived alone in their dens, or perhaps it is merely one of the normal variants of human nature – who knows? I am not a natural scientist and it is not my place to settle such questions; all I am saying is that people like Mavra are not all that uncommon. There is no need to look too far; two months ago a man called Belikov, a colleague of mine, the Greek master, died in town. You may well have heard of him. He was famous for always wearing galoshes and a warm padded coat and carrying an umbrella, even in the very finest weather. Furthermore, he kept his umbrella in a case, and his watch in a case made of gray chamois leather, and when he took out his penknife to sharpen his pencil, you saw that his penknife, too, was in its own little case. Indeed, his face seemed to be in a case as well, since he always hid it in his turned-up collar. He wore dark glasses and flannel vests, stuffed his ears with cotton, and when he got into a cab he always told the driver to put up the hood. In short, the man displayed a constant and insurmountable impulse to wrap himself in a covering, to create for himself, so to speak, a case that would isolate him and protect him from the outside world. The real world irritated him, frightened him, and kept him in a state of constant agitation. Perhaps to justify his timidity, his aversion for the actual, he always praised the past and what had never existed. Even the classical languages that he taught were, in reality, nothing more than the equivalent of the galoshes and umbrellas, which he used as a shelter from real life.

"'Oh, how sonorous, how beautiful is the Greek language!' he would say, with a mawkish expression; and, as though to prove the truth of this, he would screw up his eyes and, raising his finger into the air, intone the word 'Anthropos'!"

"Belikov even attempted to wrap his very thoughts in a case. The only things that he understood clearly were government directives and newspaper articles that forbade something. When some directive prohibited schoolboys from going out on the street after nine o'clock in the evening, or some article proclaimed physical love to be unlawful, he understood clearly and definitely. The thing was forbidden, and that was all that had to be said. In his mind, there was something dubious and disturbingly vague lurking in any sort of approval or permission. When a town drama club or reading-room or tea-shop was approved, he would shake his head and say softly:

"There's nothing wrong with that, of course; it's all very nice, but what if something unfortunate were to come of it!"

"Any sort of violation, deviation or departure from the rules sent him into a state of depression, even when, anyone would have thought, it had nothing whatsoever to do with him. If one of his colleagues was late for church, or he heard a rumor that his students had pulled some prank, or one of the mistresses was seen late one evening in the company of an officer he would get upset and voice the fear that something unfortunate might come of it. At our teachers' meetings we all felt oppressed by his caution, his pessimistic anxiety, and his invariable concern that the misbehavior he said was occurring in the male and female branches of the school and the disorder in the classroom had to be prevented from reaching the ears of the authorities, in order that something unfortunate did not come of it. And then there were his conjectures that, if Petrov were expelled from the second form and Yegorov from the fourth, it would be a very good thing indeed. And what was the result of all this? With his sighs, his dismal whining, and even the dark glasses on his little white face (you know the type of face, like a ferret's) he oppressed us into submission and we gave Petrov and Yegorov bad marks for conduct, made them serve detention and, ultimately, expelled them both.

"He would pay a visit to another teacher's house and then sit there in silence as if he were some kind of auditor or inspector. He would sit this way for an hour or two and then get up and leave. He called this 'maintaining good relationships with his colleagues.' It was obvious that coming to see us and sitting there was painful to him and that he made the effort simply because he considered it his duty as our colleague. We teachers were afraid of him. Even the headmaster feared him. The whole thing seems hard to believe: our teachers were all thinking people, people of integrity, brought up on Turgenev and Shchedrin. And yet this insignificant guy, who never went out without his galoshes and umbrella, kept us under his thumb for fifteen long years! And not only the high school! No, he had the whole town under his thumb! The ladies did not dare put on amateur theatricals on Saturdays for fear he would hear of it. Our clergy were afraid to eat meat or play cards in his presence. Because of the influence of people like Belikov, over the last ten or fifteen years, the people of the town have begun to be afraid of absolutely everything. They are afraid to talk too loudly, afraid to send letters, afraid to meet new people, afraid to read books, afraid to help the poor, afraid to teach them to read and write..."

Ivan Ivanich, wanting to say something, cleared his throat, but first he lit his pipe, and gazed at the moon. Finally, speaking slowly and deliberately, he said:

"Yes, thinking people of integrity read both Shchedrin and Turgenev, and various Buckles and that sort of stuff, yet they knuckled under and suffered in silence... that's the whole problem."

"Belikov and I lived in the same building," Burkin continued. "On the same floor; his door faced mine; I saw a lot of him, and I saw the way he lived. It was the same story: dressing-gown, nightcap, blinds, bolts, an endless series of prohibitions and restrictions of all sorts, and, of course, 'if only nothing unfortunate comes of it!' Lenten food disagreed with him, but he would not allow himself to eat meat on fast days, lest people might say Belikov did not keep the fasts. So he would eat fish cooked in butter, which, while not really a Lenten dish, was certainly more acceptable than meat... He would not keep a female servant for fear that it might give people the wrong ideas, so he hired the cook Afanasy, an old man of sixty who was a drunk and half crazy to boot, but who had once served as a military orderly and had learned to concoct something or other. This Afanasy usually stood at the door with his arms folded, sighing deeply and muttering the same phrase over and over: 'Oh yes, there are plenty of them around nowadays!'

"Belikov's bedroom was small and boxlike and his bed was shrouded with curtains. When he lay down to sleep he always pulled the bedclothes up over his head. It was hot and stuffy and the wind battered on the closed doors. There was a droning noise from the stove and the sound of sighing from the kitchen – ominous sighing. Even under his bedclothes he felt frightened. He was afraid that something bad might happen, that Afanasy might murder him or that thieves might break in, and so he had troubled dreams all night, and in the morning, when we walked to the high school together, he was glum and pale. It was obvious that the high school where we were heading and its many occupants filled his whole being with dread and aversion and that having to walk along beside me was painful to a man of his solitary temperament.

"'They are making so much noise in class these days,' he would say, as if trying to come up with a reason for his depression. 'It's just awful.'

"And, would you believe it, this Greek master, this man in a case – almost got married."

Ivan Ivanich glanced quickly into the barn, and said:

"You're kidding!"

"No, really, strange as it might seem, he almost got married. What happened was this: A new history and geography master, Mikhail Savich Kovalenko, a Ukrainian, was assigned to our school. And when he moved here, he brought his sister, Varenka, with him. He was a tall, dark young man with huge hands, and you could just see from his face that he would have a bass voice; and, indeed, he did, a voice that seemed to come out of a barrel – 'boom, boom, boom'! His sister was no longer in her first youth, about thirty, but she, too, was tall and graceful with black eyebrows and red cheeks. In short she was a real sweetheart, and so lively, so boisterous; she was always singing Ukrainian songs and laughing. The smallest thing would set her off into gales of ringing laughter – 'ha, ha, ha!' The other teachers first got to know the Kovalenkos at the headmaster's name-day party. Suddenly in the middle of our group of rigid, tense and gloomy teachers, who came to parties solely because it was expected of them, a new Aphrodite had arisen from the foam. She walked around with her hands on her hips, laughed, sang and danced. She sang with *The Winds Do Blow* with feeling, then another song, and another. We were all enchanted with her – all of us, even Belikov. He sat down by her and said with an ingratiating smile:

"'The Ukrainian language, in its delicacy and appealing resonance, is reminiscent of Ancient Greek.'

"These words flattered her and she began telling him earnestly and with feeling about the farm she had in the Gadyachsky district, where her mamma still lived, and where they grew 'such pears, such melons, such kabaks' (the Ukrainian word for pumpkin is *kabak* [the Russian word for tavern] while their word for tavern is *shinok*) and about the *borshch* they made there with tomatoes and eggplant, which was 'terribly, terribly delicious.'

"We listened and listened, and suddenly the same idea came to all of us.

"'What a good thing it would be, if could arrange to get those two married,' the headmaster's wife said to me softly.

"And for some reason all of us were reminded of the fact that our Belikov was unmarried. It suddenly seemed strange that we hadn't noticed this before, that we had completely overlooked such an important aspect of his life. What was his attitude to women? How had he resolved this vital question for himself? This had not interested us in the least until that moment; perhaps we had not even allowed ourselves to entertain the idea that a man who wears galoshes no matter what the weather and sleeps in a curtained bed could fall in love.

"'He hasn't seen forty for some time, but she must be at least thirty,' the headmaster's wife continued, developing her idea. 'It seems to me she would accept him.'

"All sorts of things are done in the provinces out of boredom, all sorts of unnecessary and nonsensical things! And that is because those things that are truly necessary are not done at all. What need was there, for instance, for us to find a wife for this Belikov, whom no one could imagine as a married man? The headmaster's wife, the inspector's wife, and all the ladies associated with our school grew livelier and even seemed better-looking, as though they had suddenly found a goal in life. The headmaster's wife would take a box at the theatre, and sitting in it we would see Varenka, with an eye-catching fan, beaming and happy, and beside her Belikov, a little bent figure, looking as though he had been extracted from his house with pincers. I would give an evening party and the ladies would insist on my inviting Belikov and Varenka. In short, the machine was set in motion. It appeared that Varenka was not averse to matrimony. She did not lead a very cheerful life with her brother. All they did from morning to night was quarrel and shout at each other. For example, Kovalenko would be coming along the street, a tall, gawky, robust young fellow in an embroidered shirt, with his hair escaping from under his cap and falling down over his forehead. In one hand he would be holding a bundle of books, in the other a thick, knotty stick. After him would come his sister, also carrying books.

"'But you haven't read it, Mikhalik!' she would be arguing loudly. 'I tell you, I swear you have not read it at all!'

"'And I tell you I have read it,' Kovalenko would cry, banging his stick on the pavement.

"'For God's sake, Mikhalik, why are you so angry? We are arguing about principles.'

"'I tell you that I have read it!' Kovalenko would shout, more loudly than ever.

"And at home, even if there was an outsider present, there was always some kind of a squabble. Such a life must have been nerve racking and, of course, she must have longed for a home of her own. Besides, there was her age to be considered; there was no time left to pick and choose. She was willing to marry anybody, even our Greek master. And, indeed, most of our young ladies don't mind whom they marry so long as they manage to get married. Be that as it may, Varenka began to show an unmistakable partiality for Belikov.

"And Belikov? Well, he used to visit Kovalenko just as he did us. He would arrive, take a seat, and remain silent. He would sit in silence and Varenka would sing *The Winds Do Blow*, or look pensively at him with her dark eyes, or suddenly go off into a peal of laughter – 'ha-ha-ha!'

"The power of suggestion plays a major role in love affairs, and an even greater one in getting married. Everybody – both his colleagues and the ladies – began assuring Belikov that he ought to get married, that there was nothing left for him in life but to get married. We all congratulated him with solemn countenances, delivering ourselves of various platitudes, such as 'marriage is a serious step.' Besides, Varenka was good-looking and interesting; she was the daughter of a Civil Councillor, and even had a farm. What was more, she was the first woman who had ever treated him in a warm and friendly manner. His head was turned and he decided that he really ought to get married."

"Well, at that point his galoshes and umbrella should have been confiscated," said Ivan Ivanich.

"Can you believe it! that turned out to be impossible. He put Varenka's portrait on his table; he kept coming to see me and talking about Varenka and family life, saying marriage was a serious step. He was frequently at Kovalenko's. And yet he did not alter his manner of life in the least. Quite the reverse: indeed, his determination to get married appeared to have a depressing effect on him. He grew thinner and paler, and seemed to retreat further and further into his case.

"'I am fond of Varvara Savishna,' he used to say to me, with a weak little smile, 'and I know that everyone ought to get married, but... you know. all this has happened so suddenly. I just need to think about it some more.'

"'What is there to think about?' I used to say to him. 'Get married – that's all.'

"'No, marriage is a serious step. One must first weigh the duties before one, the responsibilities... so that nothing unfortunate comes of it later. It worries me so much that I'm not sleeping at night. And I must confess I am afraid that she and her brother have a kind of unconventional way of thinking; they look at things, you know, strangely, and then too her disposition is very lively. A person might get married and then, for all one knows, find himself in some kind of a mess.

"And so he did not propose; he kept putting it off, to the great vexation of the headmaster's wife and all the rest of our ladies. He went on weighing the duties and responsibilities before him, and meanwhile he would go for a walk with Varenka almost every day – possibly he thought that this was mandatory in his position – and then come to see me to talk about family life. And, in all probability, in the end he would have proposed to her and would have made one of those unnecessary, stupid marriages, such as are made by thousands among us, marriages that stem from being bored and having nothing to do, if it had not been for a *kolossalische Skandal*. I must say here that Varenka's brother, Kovalenko, detested Belikov from the first day of their acquaintance; he could not stand him.

"'I don't understand,' he used to say to us, shrugging his shoulders, 'I don't understand how you can put up with that informer, that pasty face. Ugh! How can you live here? The atmosphere is stifling and disgusting! How can you call yourselves schoolmasters, teachers? What you are is petty civil servants. Your place of work is not a temple of science, but rather a bureaucracy of conformity, and it stinks like a police sentry box. No, my friends; I will stay with you a while longer and then I will go off to my farm and fish for crabs and teach the peasants. I will go, and you can stay here with your Judas – damn his soul!'

"Or he would laugh till he cried, first in a loud bass, then in a shrill, thin laugh, and ask me, waving his hands:

"'Why does he come and sit at our place? What does he want? He sits and stares.'

"He even gave Belikov a nickname, 'That Spider.' And of course we avoided talking to him of his sister's plans to marry 'That Spider.' And on one occasion, when the headmaster's wife hinted to him what a good thing it would be for his sister to settle down with a reliable, universally respected man such as Belikov, he frowned and muttered:

"'It's none of my business; let her marry a reptile if she likes. I don't like meddling in other people's business.'

"Now, just listen to what happened next. Some mischief-maker drew a caricature of Belikov walking along under his umbrella, with his trousers tucked into his galoshes and Varenka on his arm. Below the sketch was the caption 'Anthropos in love.' The artist had caught the expression on his face just perfectly – it was astonishing. He must have worked on this through more than one night, since all the teachers in both the boys' and girls' high-schools, as well as in the seminary, and all our government officials got a copy. Belikov got one, too. The caricature made a very painful impression on him.

"We had set out for school together; it was the first of May, a Sunday, and all of us, the boys and the teachers, had agreed to meet there and walk to a wood outside of town. When we set off, he was green around the gills and gloomier than a storm-cloud.

"'What wicked, mean people there are in this world!' he said, and his lips quivered.

"I even began to feel sorry for him. We were walking along, and all of a sudden – would you believe it? – Kovalenko came pedaling along on a bicycle, and behind him, on a bicycle as well, was Varenka, flushed and out of breath, but clearly in great good humor.

"'We are going on ahead,' she called. 'What lovely weather! Terribly, terribly lovely!'

"And they pedaled out of sight. Belikov's complexion went from green to white; he seemed frozen. He stopped walking and looked at me...

"'What is the meaning of this? I ask you!' he asked. 'Or perhaps I really did not see what I think I did? Since when has it been proper for school masters and ladies to ride bicycles?'

"'What is there improper about it?' I said. 'Why shouldn't they ride bicycles? Let them ride to their hearts' content.'

"'But how in the world can you say that?' he cried, amazed at my calm. 'Whatever are you saying?'

"And he was so shocked that he refused to go on and returned home.

"The next day he kept nervously rubbing his hands and wincing and it was evident from his face that he was really suffering. Indeed, for the first time in his life he actually went home before the school day was over. He ate no dinner. Towards evening he got dressed warmly, even though the weather was like summer, and dragged himself over to the Kovalenkos'. Varenka wasn't home; her brother was, however.

"'Please sit down,' Kovalenko said coldly, with a frown. He looked sleepy since he had just awoken from an after-dinner nap. He was in a very bad mood.

"After sitting in silence for ten minutes, Belikov began:

"'I have come to see you to relieve my mind. I am very, very much troubled. Some slanderer has drawn an absurd caricature of me and another individual, whom we both know well. I consider it my duty to assure you that I am no way to blame for this... I have done absolutely nothing to provide grounds for this sort of ridicule – on the contrary, I have always behaved in every respect like a complete gentleman.'

"Kovalenko just sat there, sulky and silent. Belikov waited a while and then continued quietly in a sorrowful voice.

"'There is one other thing. I have been a school master for a long time, while you have only lately entered the profession, and so I consider it my duty as your senior colleague to warn you. You have been riding a bicycle, and this kind of frivolous behavior is utterly inappropriate for an educator of youth.'

"'Why so?' asked Kovalenko in his bass voice.

"'Surely that needs no explanation, Mikhail Savich. How could it be possible you do not understand? If the teacher rides a bicycle, what can you expect the pupils to get up to? They will take to walking on their hands next! If it is not explicitly permitted by directive, then it must be considered forbidden. Yesterday, I was simply horrified! When I saw your sister, for a minute, everything actually went black before my eyes. A woman or a young lady on a bicycle – a shocking sight!'

"'What is it precisely that you want from me?'

"'All I want to do is to warn you, Mikhail Savich. You are young, you have your whole future ahead of you and you must be very, very careful about how you behave. And yet you are so negligent – so awfully negligent! You go around in an embroidered shirt; you are always carrying some kind of books around in public and now, on top of all this, there is the bicycle, too. The headmaster is sure to find out that you and your sister were riding bicycles, and then it may even reach the school superintendent... What good could possibly come of that?'

"'It's no business of anybody else's if my sister and I ride bicycles!' said Kovalenko turning crimson. 'And anyone who meddles in my private life can go straight to hell!'

"Belikov turned pale and got up.

"'If you speak to me in that tone I cannot continue,' he said. 'And I beg you never to express yourself like that about our superiors in my presence. You really ought to show more respect for the authorities.'

"'What the hell have I said that is disrespectful of the authorities?' asked Kovalenko, glaring at him furiously. 'Please leave me alone. I am an honorable man, and do not care to sully myself by talking to a gentleman like you. I can't abide informers!'

"Belikov, in extreme agitation, began hurriedly putting on his coat, with an expression of horror on his face. It was the first time in his life anyone had spoken to him so rudely.

"'You can say whatever you like,' he said, going from the hall to the stairway landing. But I must warn you that there is a possibility that someone may have overheard us. So, in order to make sure that our conversation is not misinterpreted with unfortunate consequences, I shall be compelled to inform our headmaster of what was said... in general terms. I am obliged to do so."

"'Inform him? Well, damn you, go ahead and inform him!'

"Then Kovalenko seized him from behind by the collar and gave him a push, and Belikov tumbled downstairs, his galoshes banging against the steps. The staircase was high and steep, but he reached the bottom unhurt. He got up, and touched the bridge of his nose to make sure his glasses too were intact. However, just as he was falling downstairs, Varenka had come in with two other ladies and they stood and watched him. To Belikov this was the worst thing that could have happened. I believe he would rather have broken his neck or both legs than have become an object of ridicule. Why, now the whole town would hear of it; it would reach the headmaster's ears, and then the higher authorities – and something truly unfortunate might come of it! There would be another caricature, and it would all end in his being asked to resign his position . . .

"Varenka only recognized him when he had managed to stand up. Seeing his ridiculous face, his crumpled overcoat, and his galoshes, and unaware of what had happened and thinking that it had simply been an accident, she could not restrain herself, and burst out laughing – loud enough to be heard by the entire building,

"'Ha-ha-ha!'

"And this resounding peal of laughter, this 'ha-ha-ha' was the last straw and put an end to everything: both the proposed match and Belikov's tenure on this earth. He did not hear what Varenka said to him; he saw nothing. On reaching home, the first thing he did was to remove her portrait from the table; then he went to bed and never got up again.

"Three days later Afanasy came to me to ask whether we oughtn't to send for the doctor, as there was something the matter with his master. I went in to see Belikov. He lay silent behind his curtain, covered with a quilt. If you asked him a question, he answered 'Yes' or 'No,' but did not utter another sound. He just lay there while Afanasy, gloomy and scowling, wandered around the room, sighing heavily, and smelling like a tavern.

"A month later Belikov died. We all went to his funeral – that is, both the high schools and the seminary. Now, as he was lying in his coffin, his expression was gentle, agreeable, even cheerful, as though he were glad that he had at last been put into a case that he would never have to leave again. Yes, he had attained his ideal! And, as if in his honor, it was dull, rainy weather on the day of his funeral, and we all wore galoshes and brought our umbrellas. Varenka, too, was at the funeral, and when the coffin was lowered into the grave she burst into tears. I have noticed that Ukrainian women are always either laughing or crying – nothing in between.

"It must be acknowledged that burying people like Belikov is a great pleasure. As we were returning from the cemetery we wore humble solemn faces; since no one wanted to display this feeling of pleasure – a feeling resembling what we had experienced long, long ago as children when our elders had gone out and we could run around the garden for an hour or two, enjoying complete freedom. Ah, freedom, freedom! The merest hint, the faintest hope of its possibility gives wings to the soul, does it not?

"We returned from the cemetery in high humor. But after no more than a week life returned to its previous routine, the same gloomy, oppressive, and senseless life, a life not prohibited by directive, and yet not expressly permitted. In short, things were no better. Indeed, why should they have been? Although we had buried Belikov, how many other men in cases were still left, and how many others are still to come!"

"That's the whole problem," said Ivan Ivanich as he lit his pipe.

"How many more of them are still to come!" repeated Burkin.

The schoolmaster came out of the barn. He was a short, stout man, completely bald, with a black beard down to his waist. The hunting two dogs came out with him.

"What a moon!" he said, looking upwards.

It was midnight. To the right you could see the whole village, a long street stretching away three miles into the distance. Everything was shrouded in deep silent slumber; not a movement, not a sound. It was hard to believe that nature could be so still. When on a moonlight night you see a broad village street, with its cottages, haystacks, and slumbering willows, a quiet mood comes over you. In this peace, the night shadows shelter you from toil, care and sorrow, and the street is gentle, melancholy and beautiful. Even the stars seem to look down kindly and tenderly as if there is no evil on earth and all is well. To the left it was all open fields starting from the edge of the village. You could see a long distance – to the horizon. And throughout the whole expanse of the fields, bathed in moonlight, there was no movement, no sound.

"Yes, that's the whole problem," repeated Ivan Ivanich; "and isn't the fact that we choose to live in the stuffy and crowded town, that we write useless papers, that we play Whist – aren't all those things also a a sort of case? And the fact that we spend our whole lives among useless, superficial, contentious men and silly, idle women, that we talk and listen to all sorts of nonsense – isn't that also a kind of case, too? If you like, I will tell you another very edifying story."

"No, not now; it's time to sleep," said Burkin. "You can tell me tomorrow."

They went into the barn and lay down on the hay. They had both covered themselves and were beginning to doze when they suddenly heard light footsteps – patter, patter... Some one was walking around not far from the barn, walking for a while, then stopping, and a minute later, patter, patter again... The dogs began to growl.

"That's Mavra," said Burkin.

The footsteps died away.

"They're telling lies all around us," said Ivan Ivanich, turning over, "And they call you a fool for putting up with their lying. You endure insult and humiliation and dare not openly say that you are on the side of the honest and the free, and you yourself begin to lie and smile; and all this just for the sake of a crust of bread, a warm corner or a wretched, worthless paltry rank in the civil service. No, I can't go on living like this."

"Now, that is a whole different matter, Ivan Ivanich," said the schoolmaster. "But let us go to sleep now!"

And ten minutes later Burkin was asleep. But Ivan Ivanich kept sighing and tossing from side to side. Finally, he got up, went outside again, and, sitting in the doorway, once more lit his pipe.

1898

GOOSEBERRIES

Since early morning the whole sky had been filled with rain clouds. The day was still, not hot and tedious, as it is in gray, overcast weather, when the clouds have been hanging over the fields for a long time, and you expect rain, but none comes. Ivan Ivanych, a veterinarian, and Burkin, a high-school teacher, were tired from walking. The fields seemed to stretch around them in an endless expanse. Far ahead of them they could just see the mills of the village of Mironositskoye. On the right behind the village there was a row of hills disappearing into the distance. They both knew that these hills marked the bank of the river, where there were meadows, green willows, and estates and that if you were to stand on one of these hills you could see a vast field and running through it the telegraph line and a train, which from a distance resembled a crawling caterpillar. Why, in clear weather you could even see the town from one of those hills. Now, in this still weather, when all of nature appeared gentle and pensive, both Ivan Ivanych and Burkin were filled with love for this landscape, and both were thinking how great and beautiful their country was.

"Last time we were in Prokofy's barn," said Burkin, "you were about to tell me a story."

"That's right; I was going to to tell you about my brother."

Ivan Ivanych heaved a long sigh and lit his pipe to prepare for a long speech, but, just at that moment, the rain began. And five minutes later it was already pouring steadily and who could tell when it would stop. Ivan Ivanych and Burkin stopped to think what to do; the dogs, already drenched, stood with their tails between their legs gazing at the two men adoringly.

"We must take shelter somewhere," said Burkin. "Let's go to Alyokhin's, it's close by."

"All right, let's go."

They turned aside and started walking through the mown fields, first going straight ahead, and then turning right, until they came out on the road. Soon they saw poplars and an orchard, then the red roofs of barns; then a glimpse of the river, and then finally the view opened on to a broad millpond with a mill and a white bathhouse: this was Sofino, where Alyokhin lived.

The mill wheel was turning, drowning out the sound of the rain; the dam shook. Rain-soaked horses with lowered heads were standing near their carts, and men were walking around holding sacks over themselves to keep out the rain. It was damp, muddy, and unwelcoming. This stretch of the river looked cold and forbidding. By this time, Ivan Ivanych and Burkin were feeling wet, dirty and uncomfortable all over. Their feet were heavy with mud, and as they crossed the dam and walked up to the estate barns, they were silent, as though they had stopped speaking out of anger.

They could hear the sound of a winnowing machine coming from one of the barns; its door was open, and clouds of dust were billowing out. In the doorway stood Alyokhin himself, a man of forty, tall and stout, with long hair, resembling a professor or an artist more than a landowner. He had on a white shirt badly in need of washing, belted with a rope, and long johns instead of trousers. His boots were plastered with mud and straw and his eyes and nose were black with dust. He recognized Ivan Ivanych and Burkin, and appeared delighted to see them.

"Go into the house, gentlemen," he said, smiling; "I'll be there directly, this minute."

It was a large two-story house. Alyokhin lived on the lower story, in the two rooms once inhabited by the estate bailiffs. This part of the house had arched ceilings and only small windows. It was very plainly furnished and smelled of rye bread, cheap vodka, and leather horse tackle. He rarely went into the best rooms upstairs, only when visitors came. At the house, Ivan Ivanych and Burkin were met by a maid-servant, a young woman so beautiful that they both stopped in their tracks and exchanged a glance.

"You can't imagine how happy I am to see you, my friends," said Alyokhin, following them into the front hall. "What a great surprise! Pelagea," he said, addressing the girl, "bring our guests some dry clothes to change into. And I really ought to change too. Only first I ought to go and have a wash; as far as I can remember, I haven't washed thoroughly since spring. Wouldn't you like to join me in the bathhouse? While we're there they'll be making us something to eat in the kitchen."

The lovely Pelagea, who looked very delicate and very soft, brought them towels and soap, and Alyokhin and his guests went into the bathhouse.

"Yes, it has been long time since I had a wash," he said, undressing. "I have this nice bathhouse, as you can see – my father built it – but I somehow never have time to wash."

He sat down on the ledge and soaped his long hair and his neck, and the water round him turned brown.

"So I see," said Ivan Ivanych pointedly, looking at his head.

"It's a long time since I washed…" repeated Alyokhin, embarrassed, soaping himself again. This time the water near him turned dark blue, like ink.

Ivan Ivanych went outside, jumped into the water with a loud splash, and swam in the rain. He thrashed with his arms, making waves, which set the white waterlilies bobbing up and down. He swam to the very middle of the millpond and kept diving and coming up a minute later in another place, evidently trying to touch the bottom.

"Oh, my God!" he repeating, enjoying himself "Oh, my God!" He swam over to the mill, chatted with some peasants there, then returned and floated on his back in the middle of the pond with his face to the rain. Burkin and Alyokhin were dressed and all ready to go, but he continued to swim and dive.

"Oh, my God!." he said. "Lord, have mercy!"

"That's enough, already!" Burkin shouted to him.

They went back to the house. The lamp had been lit in the big upstairs drawing-room, and Burkin and Ivan Ivanych, dressed in silk dressing-gowns and warm slippers, were sitting in armchairs; while Alyokhin, washed and combed, in a new frock coat, paced around the drawing-room, evidently enjoying the unaccustomed feeling of warmth, cleanliness, dry clothes, and light shoes. It was only after the lovely Pelagea, walking noiselessly on the carpet and smiling sweetly, had served them tea and jam on a tray – that Ivan Ivanych began to tell his story. And it seemed as though Burkin and Alyokhin were not the only listeners. The ladies and officers, young and old, who gazed down sternly and calmly from their gold frames on the wall seemed to be listening too.

"There were two of us," he began – "I, Ivan Ivanych, and my brother, Nikolay Ivanych, two years younger. I chose science and became a veterinarian, but my brother sat in a government office from the time he was nineteen. Our father, Chimsha-Gimalaysky came from a line of common soldiers, but he had risen through the ranks to be an officer. From him we inherited his newly won membership in the nobility and a small, poor estate, which, after his death was confiscated to pay off debts and legal expenses. However it had served its purpose, allowing us to spend our childhood in the freedom of the country. Like peasant children, we passed our days and nights in the fields and the woods, attending to the horses, stripping bark off trees to make shoes, fishing, and so on. And, you know, once someone, even a single time in his life has caught a perch or seen the thrushes migrating in autumn, watched the flocks gliding over the village on bright, cool days, he will never make a real townsman. He will yearn for the freedom and space of the country until the day he dies. My brother was miserable in the government office. As years passed and he sat in the same place, copying the same papers, he kept dreaming of just one thing – if only he could live in the country. And gradually this longing grew into a definite desire, into the plan to buy a little farm, a country estate somewhere on the banks of a river or a lake.

"He was a an unassuming, good-hearted fellow, and I was very fond of him, but I never really sympathized with his desire to shut himself up for the rest of his life on his own little country estate. They say that all a man needs is three *arshins* of earth.[7] But that pertains to a corpse, not a living man. And now they have also begun to say that if our intellectual classes are attracted to the land and yearn to return to the county, that is a good thing. But these country estates are really nothing more than these same three *arshins* of earth. To retreat from the city, from struggle, from the noise and bustle of life, to retreat and bury oneself on a country estate – that isn't life, it's egoism, laziness, monasticism of a sort, but monasticism without self-denial. What a man needs, is neither three *arshins* of earth nor a country estate, but the whole globe, all of nature, where he will have the space to manifest all the aspects of his unique and free spirit.

"My brother, Nikolay, sitting in his government office, dreamed of how he would eat soup made from his own cabbages, which would fill the whole yard with a mouthwatering smell, how he would dine outside, sitting on the green grass, sleep in the sun, sit for whole hours on the bench outside his gate, gazing at the fields and the forest. Pamplets on agriculture and the hints in the farmers' almanac were his delight, his favorite spiritual sustenance. He liked to read the papers too, but only the advertisements selling so many acres of arable land and meadows, complete with estate buildings, a river, an orchard, a mill and millpond. And in his imagination he pictured the path leading to the orchard, flowers and fruit, birdhouses, a pond stocked with carp , and all that stuff, you know what I mean. Each of these imaginary pictures was different, depending on the last ad he had come across, but, for some reason, every single one of them included gooseberry bushes. He could not imagine the farm of his dreams, could not picture an idyllic country retreat, without gooseberries.

"'Country life has its own particular pleasures,' he would sometimes say. 'You sit on the verandah and drink tea, and there on the pond your very own ducks are swimming, there is a wonderful smell everywhere, and... and the gooseberries are growing.'

"He used to draw maps of his imagined property, and every one of them showed the same things – (a) the main house, (b) the servants' quarters, (c) a kitchen-garden, (d) gooseberry-bushes. He lived frugally, stinting himself on food and drink. His clothes were impossible, like those of a beggar, but he kept on saving money and putting it in the bank. He grew horribly cheap. I could not bear to look at him, and I used to give him money and send him something for the holidays, but whatever I sent he stashed away. Once a man gives himself over to an idea like that, there is no doing anything with him.

"Years passed: he was transferred to another province. He was over forty, and he was still reading advertisements in the papers and saving his money. Then I heard he had gotten married. But it was only in aid of this same purpose of being able to buy a farm with gooseberries. He had married an elderly and ugly widow without having a trace of feeling for her, simply because she had a bit of money. He went on scrimping and saving after they were married, and kept her on short rations, while he put her money in the bank in his name.

"Her first husband had been a postmaster, and she had grown accustomed to rich pies and sweet liqueurs, but my brother fed her on black bread, and not enough of that. She began to to waste away from living like this, and three years later she up and passed on. And, I need hardly say, that not for a single moment did my brother ever entertain the idea that he was responsible for her death. Money, like vodka, makes a man do outlandish things. There was a merchant in our town who, right before he died, asked for a bowl of honey, coated his money and lottery tickets with it and swallowed them down – just to prevent anyone else from getting a hold of them. Once when I was inspecting cattle at the railway-station, a cattle-dealer fell under the engine and his leg got cut off. We carried him into the waiting room; the blood was flowing – it was ghastly – but he kept asking them to find his leg for him. He kept fretting about it; you see he had stashed twenty rubles in the boot he wore on that leg , and he wanted to make sure he got them back."

"You're getting sidetracked," said Burkin.

"After his wife's death," Ivan Ivanych continued after thinking for a few seconds, "my brother began looking around in earnest for an estate to buy. Of course, you can look around for five years and yet end up making a mistake – buying something that doesn't resemble your dream at all. Finally, through an agent, Nikolay bought a mortgaged estate of three hundred and thirty acres. It indeed had a main house, servants' quarters, and landscaped grounds, but no orchard, no gooseberry-bushes, and no duck-pond. True, there was a river, but the water in it was the color of coffee, because the estate was sandwiched between a a brickyard and a bonemeal plant. But this did not grieve Nikolay Ivanych all that much; he ordered twenty gooseberry-bushes, planted them, and started living the life of a country gentleman.

"Last year I went to visit him. "I'll just drop in and see what it's like,' I thought. In his letters my brother referred to his estate as 'Chumbaroklov Heath, aka Gimalayskoye.' I reached 'aka Gimalayskoye' in the heat of the afternoon. There were irrigation ditches, fences, hedges, rows of fir trees everywhere, and it was hard to figure out how to get into the yard and where to leave one's horse. I went up to the house and was greeted by a fat, reddish dog that looked more like a pig. He seemed to want to bark at me, but in the end was too lazy. My brother's cook, a fat, barelegged woman, also resembling a pig, emerged from the kitchen. She said that her master was taking a rest after dinner and I went to the bedroom to see him. He was sitting up in bed with a quilt over his knees. He had aged, and grown fat and flabby. His cheeks, nose, and mouth all seemed to be protruding from his face – he looked as though he might begin grunting into the quilt at any moment.

"We embraced each other and shed tears from joy and from sadness at the thought that we both had been young but now were gray and would soon die. He got dressed, and led me out to show me the estate.

"'Well, how's life treating you here?' I asked.

"'Oh, all right, God be thanked; it's treating me very well.'

"He was no longer a pathetic timid clerk, but a real landowner, a country gentleman. He was already fully at home in his new life; he had taken to it like a duck to water. He was eating a great deal, bathing in the bath house, and growing fat. He was already involved in land disputes with the local village commune and the factories on both sides of him; he already became terribly offended when the peasants failed to call him "your honor." He had begun to concern himself with his immortal soul in the manner of well-to-do gentlemen and did 'good works,' though he didn't simply do good works, but performed them as his duty as a man of property. What were they, these good works? Well, he dosed the sick peasants, no matter what their illness, with bicarbonate and castor oil, and on his name day he commissioned prayers of gratitude in the village, and then provided the villagers with a half-*vedro*[23] of vodka, thinking this was the thing to do. Oh, those ghastly half-*vedros*! One day a fat landowner hauls the peasants off to the sheriff because their cattle trampled his crops, and next day, to celebrate some holiday, he treats them to a half-*vedro* of vodka, and they drink and shout 'Hurrah!' and, when they are good and drunk, they bow down to the ground before him. For the average Russian, an improvement in living standard gives rise to the most arrogant conceit. Nikolay Ivanych, who, when he worked at the government office, hadn't dared to have a single opinion of his own, now thought that everything he said was was nothing less than the gospel truth, and he delivered his opinions in the tones of a government minister: 'Education is essential, but for our peasants it is premature.' 'Corporal punishment is harmful as a rule, but in some cases it is necessary and there is no substitute for it.'

"'I understand our peasants and I know how to deal with them,' he would say. 'The peasants like me. All I need to do is crook my finger, and they'll do whatever I want them to.'

"And all this, please note, was uttered with a wise, benevolent smile. He would repeat over and over, phrases of the type 'We noblemen,' 'I, as a noble,' evidently having forgotten that that our grandfather had been a peasant, and our father a common soldier. Even our ridiculous surname, Chimsha-Gimalaysky, now seemed to him resonant, distinguished, and very pleasant to the ear.

"But what I wanted to talk about was not him so much, but me, myself. I want to tell you about the change that took place in me during the brief hours I spent at his country place. In the evening, when we were drinking tea, the cook brought us a whole bowl full of gooseberries. These had not been bought somewhere, but were my brother's own gooseberries, the very first harvest since his bushes were planted. Nikolay Ivanych began to laugh and for a moment gazed at the gooseberries in silence with tears in his eyes; he could not speak for emotion. Then he put one gooseberry in his mouth, looked at me with the triumph of a child who has at last managed to get hold of the toy of his dreams, and said:

"'How delicious!'

"And he ate them greedily, continually repeating, 'Ah, how delicious! Do try some!'

"They were hard and sour, but, as Pushkin says, 'falsehood that uplifts us is dearer than a host of truths.' I was looking at a happy man, whose cherished dream had incontrovertibly come true, who had achieved his goal in life, who had gotten what he wanted, who was completely satisfied with his fate and with himself. For some reason, my thinking about human happiness has always contained an element of melancholy; and now, at the sight of this completely happy man, I was overcome by a painful emotion, close to despair. I passed an awful night. My bed had been made up in the room next to my brother's bedroom, and I could hear that he was wakeful, and kept getting out of bed and walking over to the bowl of gooseberries and taking yet one more berry. The idea came to me that, truly, there were a huge number of satisfied, happy people in the world! What a force for oppression! You look at this life, at the arrogance and idleness of those with power, the ignorance and the animal-like existence of the weak. Everywhere there is inconceivable poverty, overcrowding, degeneracy, drunkenness, hypocrisy, lying… And yet it is calm and quiet in all the houses, on all the streets. Of the fifty thousand people living in a town, there is not one who will stand up and shout, who will express his outrage aloud. We see the people who go to market to buy food, who eat by day and sleep by night, who speak only of superficial things, who get married, grow old, and cheerfully cart their dead off to the cemetery. But we do not see and we do not hear those who suffer, and what is terrible in life goes on somewhere behind the scenes. Everything is quiet and peaceful, and the only protest comes from voiceless statistics: the number of people who have gone mad, the number of *vedros* of vodka drunk, the number of children dead from malnutrition… And this system is evidently necessary; evidently the happy person is only able to feel comfortable because the miserable bear their burdens in silence. Without such silence, happiness would be impossible. It's a case of universal hypnosis. Outside the door of every happy, contented person there should be someone standing and pounding with a hammer, in order to remind him that there are people in misery, that however happy he may be now, sooner or later life will show him her claws. Trouble will find him – disease, poverty, losses, but no one will see or hear, just as now he neither sees nor hears others. But there is no man with a hammer; the happy person lives his life, and trivial daily cares agitate him but faintly, like the wind in the aspen tree – and all is well.

"That night I realized that I, too, was one of those happy and contented people," Ivan Ivanych continued, getting up from his chair. "At the dinner table and while hunting, I too liked to tell people how to live, what to believe and how best to deal with the peasantry. I, too, used to say that knowledge is power, and education is essential, but for common people learning how to read and write is enough for the present. 'Freedom is a universal good,' I would say, 'and denying it to people is like denying them air, but we must wait a little longer.' Yes, I used to talk like that, and now I ask, 'For the sake of what should we wait?'" Ivan Ivanych asked, glaring angrily at Burkin. "Why wait, I ask you? What reason can there possibly be for waiting? They tell me that what is needed can't be provided all at once; that every idea can be implemented in real life only gradually, in its own good time. Who says? Where is the proof that this is correct? You will answer by referring to the natural order of things, the conformity of all phenomena to certain laws; but where is there order and conformity in the fact that I, a living, thinking man, must stand at the lip of a chasm and wait for it to seal itself closed, or to fill up with silt, when perhaps I could simply leap over it or build a bridge across it? And again I ask, 'wait, for what purpose? Should I wait till we no longer have the strength to continue living. Yet, in the meantime people must live and want to live!'

"I left my brother's place early in the morning, and ever since then I have found it unbearable to be in town. I am oppressed by its peace and quiet; I am afraid to look in windows, for there is no spectacle more painful to me now than the sight of a happy family sitting round the table drinking tea. I am old and unfit for struggle; I am not even capable of hatred; I can only grieve internally, feel annoyed or vexed; and yet at night my head is on fire with the rush of ideas, and I cannot sleep… Ah, if I were only young!"

In his agitation, Ivan Ivanych paced back and forth between one corner of the room and another, repeating "If I were only young!"

He suddenly went up to Alyokhin and began pressing first one of his hands and then the other.

"Pavel Konstantinych," he said in an imploring voice, "don't subside into calm, don't let yourself be put to sleep! While you are young, strong, and self-confident, you must work tirelessly for good! There is no such thing as happiness, and indeed there ought not to be; but if life has a meaning and an object, that meaning and object must not be our personal happiness, but something greater and more rational. Work for good!"

And Ivan Ivanych said all this with a pathetic, imploring smile, as though he were begging for something for himself.

After this all three men sat in armchairs at different corners of the drawing room and said nothing. Ivan Ivanych's story had not satisfied either Burkin or Alyokhin. The generals and ladies, gazing down from their gilt frames and appearing, in the dusk, to be alive, had found it boring to listen to a story about a poor clerk who ate gooseberries. For some reason, they had wanted to speak and hear about people from high society, especially ladies. But the fact that they were sitting in a drawing-room where everything – the chandeliers in their dustcovers, the arm-chairs, and the carpet underfoot – reminded them that they, the very people who were now looking down from their frames, had once moved about, and had sat and drunk tea in this room, where the lovely Pelagea was now entering noiselessly, was better than any story.

Alyokhin was terribly sleepy; he had gotten up early, before three o'clock in the morning, to see to his work, and now his eyes were closing. Yet he was afraid his visitors might say something interesting in his absence, so he stayed. Whether what Ivan Ivanych had just said was rational and correct, mattered little to him. His guests had been speaking about something other than groats, or hay, or tar, something that had no direct bearing on his life, and he was pleased and wanted them to go on.

"It's bed-time, though," said Burkin, standing up. "Permit me to wish you good night."

Alyokhin said good night and went to his quarters downstairs, while the guests remained upstairs. They had been allocated a large room that contained two old, wooden beds decorated with carvings, and, in the corner, an ivory crucifix. The big, cool beds, made up by the lovely Pelagea, smelt pleasantly of clean linens.

Ivan Ivanych undressed in silence and got into bed.

"Lord, forgive us sinners!" he said, and drew the cover up over his head.

His pipe, lying on the table, smelled strongly of stale tobacco, and Burkin could not sleep for a long while, unable to figure out where the unpleasant smell was coming from.

Rain knocked on the window panes all night.

1898

ABOUT LOVE

Next day at lunch the guests were served some very tasty pies, crayfish, and mutton cutlets. While they were eating, Nikanor, the cook, came in to ask what they would like for dinner. He was a man of medium height with a puffy face and small eyes. He was clean shaven, but it looked as though the hair on his face had been plucked out rather than shaved off.

Alyokhin told his visitors that the beautiful Pelagea was in love with this cook. Since Nikanor drank heavily and tended to get violent, she did not want to marry him, but was willing simply to live with him. He, however, was very religious, and his convictions would not allow him to live in sin. He demanded that she marry him and would hear of nothing else, and when he got drunk he used to curse and threaten her and even beat her. Whenever this happened she hid upstairs, sobbing, and on such occasions Alyokhin and his servants stayed in the house so they could protect her if necessary.

The men began to discuss love.

"The question of what gives rise to love," remarked Alyokhin, "for example, why Pelagea doesn't love somebody more like herself in character and appearance, but instead falls for Nikanor, with his ugly snout (that's what we all call him, 'Snout') or how much personal happiness matters to love – the answers to such questions are completely unknown. Everyone is free to think whatever he wants about them. So far only one indisputable truth has been spoken about love: 'This is a great mystery.' Everything else that has ever been written or said about love is not an answer or a solution, but only a restatement of questions that still remain unanswered. The explanation that would seem to fit one case does not apply in a dozen others, and the very best thing, to my mind, would be to explain every case individually without attempting to generalize. We ought, as the doctors say, to individualize each case."

"Absolutely right," Burkin assented.

"We Russians, as an educated people, are partial to questions that cannot be answered. Love is normally poeticized, decorated with roses and nightingales. And we Russians decorate our love with these portentous questions, and, furthermore, always choose to dwell on the least interesting among them. When I was a student in Moscow, I had a mistress, a charming woman, and every time I held her in my arms she was thinking about how much housekeeping money I would give her that month and what the going price for a pound of beef was. In the same way, when we are in love, we never cease asking ourselves questions of a certain type: whether our love is honorable or dishonorable, rational or stupid, what it is leading to, and so on. Whether this is a good thing or not I don't know, but I do know that it gets in the way and makes us dissatisfied and irritable."

These words seemed to be leading up to a story he wanted to tell. People who live alone always have something stored up inside that they are eager to talk about. In town, bachelors visit the public baths and restaurants in order to talk and sometimes tell the bath attendants and waiters the most interesting stories. People who live in the country, as a rule, unburden themselves to their houseguests. Outside the window the sky was gray, the trees were drenched with rain; in this weather the men had no wish to leave the house, and so there was nothing left to do but to tell and listen to stories.

"I have lived at Sofino and occupied myself with farming for quite a long time," Alyokhin began, "ever since I left the University. My education prepared me to do anything but manual labor and my temperament predisposes me to intellectual pursuits, but when I came home from the university, there was a large debt outstanding on our estate, which my father had mortgaged partially to pay for my expensive education. I decided that I would not leave here until I had paid off this debt. I made this resolve and began working, I confess, not without some feeling of distaste. The soil here is not very fertile and, to keep from losing money on the crops, you either have to rely on the labor of serfs or hired hands (which is virtually the same thing) or work the land the way the peasants do, that is work in the field yourself with your family. There is no middle ground. But at first I did not bother with such fine distinctions. I did not leave a clod of earth unturned; I rounded up all the peasants, men and women both, from the neighboring villages and put them to work. And work we did; at a furious pace. I myself plowed and sowed and reaped. And I was bored every minute of the time, screwing up my face fastidiously like a cat forced by hunger to eat cucumbers from the kitchen-garden. My whole body ached, and I was continually falling asleep on my feet. At the beginning I thought I could easily live this life of hard labor while retaining my cultured habits, if I could only maintain a certain external order in my life. Thus, I established myself upstairs here in the best rooms, and had the servants bring my coffee and liqueur to me up there after lunch and dinner. I would read *Chronicle of Europe* every night before I went to sleep. But one day our priest, Father Ivan, dropped by and polished off my entire stock of liqueur at a single go. Then I gave my copies of *Chronicle of Europe* to the priest's daughters, since in summer, especially during haymaking, I never made it to my bed at all, but fell asleep in a sledge in the barn, or somewhere in the forester's lodge. What chance did I have to read? Little by little I moved downstairs and began dining in the servants' kitchen, and now nothing is left of my former luxury but the servants I cannot bear to let go because they were in my father's service.

"Not long after I settled here, I was made an honorary member of the magistrate's court. From time to time I would have to go into town to attend sessions of the district congress or court, which made a pleasant break for me. When you spend two or three months cooped up in the country without going anywhere, especially in the winter, you start to long for the sight of a black frock coat. And these sessions showed me frock-coats, and uniforms, and dress-coats, too. The members of the court were lawyers, educated men with whom I could have real discussions. After sleeping in the sledge and eating my meals in the kitchen, to sit in an armchair in clean linen and dress shoes, with a chain of office around my neck, was quite a luxury!

I received a warm welcome in the town and was very eager to make new acquaintances. Of all those I met, the one I knew and, to tell the truth, liked the best was Luganovich, the vice-president of the court. I think both of you know him, the nicest fellow you'd ever hope to meet. You remember the famous arson case we had? Well, the preliminary investigation lasted two days. The whole court was exhausted. Luganovich looked at me and said:

"'You know what, why don't you come and have dinner at my house?'

"This was unexpected, since my acquaintance with Luganovich had been strictly professional and I had never been to his house before. I went to my hotel room and took a minute or two to change my clothes and off I went to dinner. And there I had the opportunity to get to know Anna Alexeyevna, Luganovich's wife. At that time she was still very young, no more than twenty-two; her first child had been born only six months before. It is all a thing of the past; and now I find it difficult to define what exactly there was about her that I found so exceptional, that attracted me so much. But that time, at that first dinner, the reasons were overwhelmingly clear to me. I saw a young women who was beautiful, good-hearted, intelligent and enchanting, whose equal I had never before encountered. Immediately I felt I had some sort of bond with her. She seemed familiar to me, as if I had seen that face, those friendly, intelligent eyes, some time during my childhood; perhaps in the album my mother kept on her dresser.

"Four Jews had been charged with arson, and they had been tried as a criminal gang, which I thought was completely unfounded. During dinner my mind was still on this case that had disturbed me a great deal; I can't tell you what I myself said, but I do remember that Anna Alexeyevna kept shaking her head and saying to her husband:

"'Dmitry, how could this have happened?'

"Luganovich is a good soul, but he is one of those naive people who are firmly of the opinion that once someone has been brought before a court, he must be guilty, and that the only way it is permissible to question the verdict is on paper, following due legal procedures, and not over dinner in a private conversation. "'Well, you and I, for example are innocent of arson,' he said mildly, 'and so no one has tried us for it or sent us to prison.'

"And both of them – husband and wife – kept urging me to have more to eat and drink. Certain trifling details that I observed, the way they made the coffee together, for instance, and the way they understood each other's thoughts before a sentence was completed, made me think that that they had a close and happy marriage and were pleased to have visitors. After dinner they played a duet on the piano; then it got dark, and I went home. That was in early spring.

"I spent the entire following summer at Sofino without a break and had no time to think about life in town, but I carried the memory of the slender, fair-haired woman with me throughout that period. I did not really think about her, but it was as though a faint shadow of her was always present in my mind.

"In late autumn I attended a theatrical performance in town, a charity benefit. I had been invited to visit the governor's box during the intermission and when I did, I saw Anna Alexeyevna sitting beside the governor's wife. Once again I had the sudden, overwhelming impression of beauty and warm, understanding eyes, and again the same feeling that there was a bond between us. We sat side by side for a while and then went out into the lobby.

"'You've grown thinner,' she said; 'have you been ill?'

"'Yes, I've had rheumatism in my shoulder, and in rainy weather I sleep badly.'

"'You look run down. In the spring, when you came to dinner, you were younger, more confident. You were full of eagerness then, and talked a great deal; you were very interesting, and I confess you made quite an impression on me. For some reason you often popped into my memory during the summer, and as I was getting ready for the theatre today I thought I was likely to see you.'

"And she laughed.

"'But you look run down today,' she repeated; 'it makes you seem older.'

"The next day I lunched at the Luganoviches'. After lunch they were going to drive to their summer place, in order to make arrangements for the winter, and I accompanied them. We returned to town together, and, at midnight I was drinking tea with them in quiet domestic surroundings while the fire glowed, and the young mother kept leaving the room to make sure her little girl was asleep. And after that, when I went to town, I never failed to visit the Luganoviches. They grew used to me, and I grew used to them. As a rule I would enter their house unannounced, like one of the family.

"'Who is there?' she would call from one of the inner rooms far off, in the light drawl that I found so attractive.

"'It's Pavel Konstantinovich,' the maid or nanny would answer.

"Anna Alexeyevna would come out to me with a worried face, and would ask me every time, 'Why has it been so long since you were here? Did something happen?'

"Her eyes, the graceful, aristocratic looking hand that she offered me, her everyday dress, the way she did her hair, her voice, her step, always produced the same impression on me, that there was something new and extraordinary in my life, something important. We would talk for hours, or we would sit in silence, each thinking their own thoughts, or she would play the piano for me. If I found no one at home I stayed and waited, chatting with the nanny, playing with the child, or lying on the Turkish sofa in the study reading a newspaper. When Anna Alexeyevna came back I would meet her in the front hall and take her parcels from her; and, for some reason, I would carry those parcels every time with the kind of great love and great solemnity a boy would feel.

"There is a proverb that says that, if a peasant woman has nothing to fret over, she goes out and buys a pig. So too it seemed that the Luganoviches had had nothing to fret over, so they made friends with me. If I did not come to town for a while, they were sure I was sick or something else had happened to me, and they both became extremely anxious. They worried that I, an educated man with a knowledge of languages, instead of devoting myself to science or literary pursuits, was living in the country, running like a squirrel in a wheel, working like a dog, and never had a penny to show for it. They imagined that I was unhappy and that I only talked, laughed, and ate to conceal my suffering. Even when I was enjoying myself and did indeed feel happy, I was aware of their searching eyes fixed upon me. They were particularly touching when I really was in a bad state, when a creditor was pressuring me or I did not have the money to pay my mortgage on time. The two of them, husband and wife, would go off to the window and whisper together, then Luganovitch would come to me and say with a serious expression on his face:

"'If you currently are in need of some money, Pavel Konstantinovich, my wife and I beg you not to hesitate to borrow from us.'

"And he would blush to his ears with emotion. Other times, after they had whispered in the same way at the window, he would come up to me, again with red ears, and say:

"'My wife and I earnestly beg you to accept this present.'

"And he would give me cuff links, a cigarette case, or a lamp, and in return I would send them game, butter, and flowers from the country. I should mention here that they both had considerable money of their own. When I had first moved here, I often borrowed money, and was not very fastidious about it — I borrowed wherever I could — but nothing in the world would have induced me to borrow from the Luganoviches. But why talk of money?

"I was indeed unhappy. In my house, in the barn, I was always thinking about her. I kept trying to figure out why a beautiful, intelligent young woman would marry someone who was not particularly interesting and nearly an old man (her husband was past forty) and bear his children. I would ponder the mystery of how this undistinguished though good-hearted and straightforward man, this man with a simple outlook on life, whose opinions were so boring and commonsensical, who sat out dances at parties among the solid citizens, listless and unsought after, with a passive indifferent expression as if he were at a business meeting, could yet believe in his right to be happy, to have children with her. I kept trying to understand why she had met him first, and not me, and how such a terrible mistake had been allowed to occur in our lives.

"And each time I went into town I could see from her eyes that she was expecting me, and indeed she would confess to me she had had a strange feeling all that day and had guessed that I would be coming. We would alternate long periods of talking with periods of silence, but we never acknowledged our love for each other, timidly and jealously concealing it. We were afraid of everything that might bring our secret out in the open even to ourselves. I loved her tenderly, deeply, but I kept analyzing the situation and asking myself what dire repercussions our love might have if we failed to find the strength to fight against it. My love was so gentle and so sad; and I could not conceive of it being the means for the abrupt interruption of the calm happy life of her husband and children, and this whole household in which everyone loved and trusted me. How could this be honorable? She would have to go away with me, but where? Where could I take her? It would have been something else entirely if I had had been leading a wonderful, interesting life – if, for instance, I had been working for the emancipation of my country, or was a celebrated scientist, artist or painter; but I simply would be taking her from one unexceptional prosaic life to another, equally as prosaic, if not more so. And how long would our happiness last? What would happen to her if I were to become ill, or die, or if we simply stopped loving each other?

"And she apparently had been thinking along similar lines. She considered her husband, her children, and her mother, who loved Luganovich like a son. If she had given in to her feelings for me, she would either have had to lie, or else tell the truth, and in her position either alternative would have been equally terrible and painful. And, too, she was tormented by the question of whether her love would bring me happiness. Would she not complicate my life, which, as it was, was hard enough and full of all sorts of trouble? She imagined that she was not young enough for me, that she was not hardworking or energetic enough to begin a new life, and she often talked to her husband about how I needed to marry a girl of intelligence and character who would be a good homemaker and helpmate to me – and then she would immediately add that it if you searched the whole town you would be unlikely to find even one such girl.

"Meanwhile the years were passing. Anna Alexeyevna already had two children. When I arrived at the Luganoviches' the servants smiled cordially, the children shouted that Uncle Pavel Konstantinovich had come, and hung on my neck; everyone was delighted. They did not understand what was going on in my soul, and thought that I, too, was happy. Everyone looked on me as a noble being. The adults and children alike felt that a noble being was walking about their rooms, and this gave a special charm to their manner towards me, as though my presence there made their lives, too, purer and more beautiful. Anna Alexeyevna and I used to go to the theatre together; we always went on foot and sat side by side in the stalls, our shoulders touching. I would take the opera glass from her hands without a word, and I would feel at that minute that we were truly joined together, that she was mine, that we could not live without each other. Yet, through some strange misunderstanding, each time we emerged from the theatre we said goodbye and parted as though we were mere acquaintances. People in town had already begun to talk about us, saying God knows what, but there was not a word of truth in any of it!

"After some years passed, Anna Alexeyevna started to go away on frequent visits to her mother or sister; and began to be moody. At times she suffered, feeling that she was not satisfied with her life, and even that her life was ruined. And at those times she felt reluctant to be in the presence of her husband and children. She had begun to seek treatment for depression.

"We maintained our silence, and in the presence of outsiders she displayed a strange irritation with me: she disagreed with whatever I said and if I got into a dispute she would always take the other person's side. If I dropped something, she would say coldly:

"'I congratulate you.'

"If I forgot to bring along the opera-glasses when we went to the theatre, she would say afterwards:

"'I just knew you would forget them.'

"Luckily or unluckily, there is nothing in our lives that does not eventually come to an end. The time came when we had to part.

Luganovich had been appointed chairman of a court in one of the western provinces. They had to sell their furniture, their horses, and their summer house. We drove out to the summer house, and on the way back, when we turned around for one last look at the garden and the green roof, we were all sad and I realized that it was not just the house I was saying goodbye to. It had been decided that, in late August, Anna Alexeyevna would go off to the Crimea, at her doctor's recommendation, and Luganovich and the children would set off for the western province a little after that.

"A large crowd turned out to see Anna Alexeyevna off. When she had already said goodbye to her husband and her children and there was only a minute left before the third bell, I ran into her compartment to put a basket, which she had almost forgotten, on the rack, and I too had to say goodbye. When our eyes met in the compartment, our will power deserted us both; I took her in my arms, she pressed her face to my chest and wept, I kissed her face, her shoulders, and her hands wet with tears – oh, how wretched we were! – I confessed my love for her, and, with a burning pain in my heart, I realized how unnecessary, petty, and illusory was everything that had gotten in the way of our love. I understood that when you love you must either base all the decisions and judgments you make about that love on what is its most exalted aspect, on that which is more important than happiness or unhappiness, sin or virtue in their accepted meaning, or you must refrain entirely from making decisions and judgments.

"I kissed her for the last time, pressed her hand, and we parted forever. The train had already started. I went into the next compartment – it was empty – and sat there weeping until we reached the next station. Then I walked home to Sofino…"

While Alyokhin was telling his story, the rain stopped and the sun came out. Burkin and Ivan Ivanich went out onto the balcony, from which there was a beautiful view over the garden and the mill pond, which now was shining in the sun like a mirror. They admired

it, and at the same time they were sorry that this man with the kind, understanding eyes, who had told them this story with such genuine feeling, should be rushing round and round this huge estate like a squirrel in a wheel instead of devoting himself to science or something else that would have made his life more pleasant; and they thought what a sorrowful face Anna Alexeyevna must have had when he said goodbye to her in the railway carriage and kissed her face and shoulders. Both of them had met her in the town, and Burkin was acquainted with her and thought her beautiful.

1898

THE BRIDE

I

It was ten o'clock in the evening and a full moon shone over the garden. In the Shumins' house an evening service ordered by grandma Marfa Mikhailovna had just ended, and now Nadya – she had stepped out into the garden for a moment – could see that the table in the dining room was being covered with appetizers, and that grandma was bustling about in her splendid silk dress; Father Andrey, a chief priest at the cathedral, was talking to Nadya's mother, Nina Ivanovna, who, in the evening light that shone through the window, for some reason looked very young; Andrey Andreyich, Father Andrey's son, was standing nearby, listening attentively.

It was still and cool in the garden, and dark, peaceful shadows lay on the ground. There was a sound of frogs croaking, far, very far away, beyond the town. There was a feeling of May, sweet May! Breathing deeply, one liked to think that not here but somewhere under the heavens, above the trees, far off beyond the town, in the fields and the woods, one's spring life was unfolding – a life that was mysterious,

lovely, rich and holy, beyond the understanding of weak, sinful man. And for some reason one wanted to cry.

She, Nadya, was already twenty-three. Ever since she was sixteen she had passionately dreamed of marriage and now at last she was engaged to Andrey Andreyich, the young man who stood on the other side of the window; she liked him, the wedding was fixed for July 7, and yet there was no joy in her heart, she slept badly at night, happiness had disappeared... Through the open windows of the basement, where the kitchen was, came the sounds of hurrying, the clatter of knives, the banging of the swing door; it smelled of roast turkey and pickled cherries. And for some reason it seemed like this was what her whole life would be like – unchanging, unending.

Someone came out of the house and stood on the steps; it was Alexander Timofeyich, or, simply, Sasha, the guest who had come from Moscow ten days before. Years ago a distant relation of grandmother's – a gentleman's widow named Marya Petrovna, a thin, sickly little woman who had sunk into poverty – used to come to the house to ask for assistance. She had a son, Sasha. For some reason it was said that he was a talented artist, and when his mother died, Nadya's grandmother had, for the salvation of her soul, sent him to the Komissarovsky School1 in Moscow; two years later he transferred to the school of painting, spent nearly fifteen years there, and only just managed to scrape through the exit exams in the architecture department. He did not set up as an architect, however, but took a job with a Moscow lithographer. He came home almost every year, usually very ill, to stay with Nadya's grandmother in order to rest and recover.

He now wore a buttoned-up frock coat and shabby canvas trousers crumpled into creases at the bottoms. And his shirt had not been ironed and he had the look of not being altogether fresh. He was very thin, with big eyes, long thin fingers and a swarthy, bearded face, and yet he was handsome. He was like one of the family to the Shumins,

and felt at home in their house. And the room where he lived here had long since been called Sasha's room.

Standing on the steps he saw Nadya, and went up to her.

"It's nice here at your place," he said.

"Of course it's nice, you ought to stay here till the autumn."

"Yes, I expect it will come to that. Perhaps I shall stay with you till September."

He laughed for no reason, and sat down beside her.

"I'm sitting and watching my mother from out here," Nadya said. "From here, she looks so young! My mother has her weaknesses, of course," she added, after a pause, "but still, she is an exceptional woman."

"Yes, she is very nice . . ." Sasha agreed. "Your mother, in her own way of course, is a very good and sweet woman, but . . . how shall I put it? I went early this morning into your kitchen and there I found four servants sleeping on the floor, no beds, and rags for bedding, stench, bugs, cockroaches… Everything is just as it was twenty years ago, no change at all. Well, grandmother, God bless her, what else can you expect of grandmother? But your mother speaks French, you know, and acts in private theatricals. One would think she might understand."

As Sasha talked, he stretched two long, wasted fingers before his listener's face.

"I'm so unaccustomed to things here, it all seems somehow absurd," he went on. "Damned if I can figure it out. Nobody ever does anything. Your mother spends the whole day walking about like a duchess, grandmother does nothing either, nor you either. And your fiancé Andrey Andreyich never does anything either."

Nadya had heard this the year before and, it seemed, the year before that too, and she knew that Sasha could not discuss anything else, and while this had previously amused her, now for some reason she was annoyed.

"That's all stale, and I've been sick of it for ages," she said and got up. "You should think of something a little newer."

He laughed and got up too, and they went together toward the house. Beside him she – tall, beautiful, and graceful – looked rather healthy and smartly dressed; she could sense this and felt sorry for him and for some reason awkward.

"And you say a great deal you should not," she said. "You've just been talking about my Andrey, but you don't even know him."

"'My Andrey'… Never mind him, with your Andrey! It's your youth I am sorry for."

When they entered the hall, everyone was already sitting down to supper. Grandmother, or Granny as she was called in the household, was very stout, plain-looking, with bushy eyebrows and a little moustache, and talked loudly. From her voice and manner of speaking it was clear that she was in charge in the household. She owned rows of shops in the market and the ancient house with its columns and garden, yet every morning she prayed that God might save her from ruin, crying all the while. Her daughter-in-law, Nadya's mother, Nina Ivanovna, was fair-haired, tightly-corsetted, wore a pince-nez and had diamonds on every finger. Father Andrey was a lean, toothless old man whose face always looked as if he were about to say something amusing. And his son, Andrey Andreyich, was a stout, handsome young man with curly hair, who looked like an artist or an actor. The three of them were talking of hypnotism.

"You will get well in a week here," said Granny, addressing Sasha. "You just have to eat more. Do you know what you look like!" she sighed. "You've become dreadful! You are a real prodigal son, that's what you are."

"After wasting his father's substance in riotous living," said Father Andrey slowly, his eyes laughing. "He fed with senseless beasts."

"I like my dad," said Andrey Andreyich, touching his father on the shoulder. "He is a splendid old fellow, a dear old fellow."

Everyone fell silent. Sasha suddenly burst out laughing and put his dinner napkin to his mouth.

"So you believe in hypnotism?" said Father Andrey to Nina Ivanovna.

"I cannot, of course, assert that I believe," answered Nina Ivanovna, assuming a very serious, even severe, expression; "but I must admit that there is much that is mysterious and incomprehensible in nature."

"I quite agree with you, though I must add that faith significantly limits for us the realm of the mysterious."

A large, very fat turkey was served. Father Andrey and Nina Ivanovna continued their conversation. Nina Ivanovna's diamonds glittered on her fingers, then tears began to glitter in her eyes and she grew excited.

"Though I cannot venture to argue with you," she said, "you must admit there are so many insoluble riddles in life!"

"Not one, I assure you."

After supper Andrey Andreyich played the fiddle and Nina Ivanovna accompanied him on the piano. Ten years before, he had taken his degree at the university in the Faculty of Arts, but had never held any post, had no definite work, and only from time to time took part in concerts for charity; but in the town he was regarded as a musician.

Andrey Andreyich played; they all listened in silence. The samovar simmered quietly on the table and no one but Sasha was drinking tea. Then, when it struck twelve, a violin string suddenly broke; everyone laughed, bustled about, and began saying goodbye.

After seeing her fiancé out, Nadya went upstairs where she lived with her mother (the lower story was occupied by grandmother). Downstairs, in the dining room, they began putting out the lights, yet Sasha still sat about drinking tea. He always spent a long time over tea, in the Moscow style, drinking as much as seven glasses at a time. For a long time after Nadya had undressed and gone to bed she could hear the servants clearing away downstairs and Granny talking angrily.

Finally everything quieted, and the only thing that could be heard was Sasha's occasional bass cough in his room below.

II

When Nadya woke up it must have been about two o'clock, it was beginning to get light. A watchman was tapping somewhere far away.2 She did not feel like sleeping, and her bed felt very soft and uncomfortable. Nadya, as she had done every night in May, sat up in her bed and started thinking. Her thoughts were the same as they had been the night before, useless, persistent thoughts, always the same, of how Andrey Andreyich had begun courting her and had made her an offer, how she had accepted him and then little by little had come to appreciate this good, intelligent man. But now for some reason, when there was hardly a month left until the wedding, she began to feel a dread and restlessness, as though before her loomed something vague and oppressive.

"Tick-tock, tick-tock..." the watchman lazily tapped. "...Tick-tock."

Through the big, old-fashioned window she could see the garden and in the distance lilac bushes in full flower, drowsy and lifeless from the cold; a thick white mist was floating softly up to the lilac, trying to cover it. Sleepy rooks were cawing in the far-away trees.

"Oh Lord, why is my heart so heavy?"

Perhaps every girl felt the same before her wedding. Who knows! Or was it Sasha's influence? But for several years Sasha had been repeating the same thing, like a copybook, and when he talked he seemed naïve and queer. But why could she not get Sasha out of her head? Why?

The watchman had long since stopped tapping. The birds were twittering under the windows and the mist had disappeared from the garden. Everything was lit up by the spring sunshine as by a smile. Soon the whole garden, warmed and caressed by the sun, returned to life, and dewdrops glittered like diamonds on the leaves; that morning the old neglected garden looked young and festive.

Granny was already awake. Sasha began to cough in his husky bass. There was the sound from downstairs of the setting up of the samovar and the moving of chairs.

The hours passed slowly, Nadya had been up and walking about the garden for a long time, yet still the morning dragged on.

At last Nina Ivanovna appeared, her face tear-stained, carrying a glass of mineral water. She was interested in spiritualism and homeopathy, read a great deal, was fond of talking of the doubts to which she was subject, and to Nadya this all seemed to contain a deep mysterious significance. Now Nadya kissed her mother and walked beside her.

"What have you been crying about, mother?" she asked.

"Last night I was reading a story about an old man and his daughter. The old man serves in some office and his chief falls in love with his daughter. I have not finished it, but there was a passage where it was hard to hold back the tears," Nina Ivanovna said, sipped from her glass. "I thought of it this morning and again began to cry."

"I have been so depressed for so long," Nadya said after a pause. "Why is it I don't sleep at night!"

"I don't know, dear. When I can't sleep I shut my eyes very tightly, like this, and picture Anna Karenina3 moving about and talking, or something historical, from the ancient world. . . ."

Nadya felt her mother did not understand her, that she was incapable of understanding her. It was the first time in her life she had felt this way, and it positively frightened her; it made her want to hide herself, and she went to her room.

At two o'clock they sat down to dinner. It was Wednesday, a fast day, and so fasting *borshch* and bream with *kasha* were set before grandmother.4

To tease grandmother, Sasha ate his non-fasting soup as well as the fasting *borshch*. He made jokes through the entire dinner, but his jests were labored and invariably with a moral undertone. It was especially unfunny when, before making some witty remark, he raised his long, thin, deathly fingers. All the more so when one remembered that he was very ill and was probably not much longer for this world. He was so emaciated that it saddened one to the verge of tears.

After dinner, grandmother went to her room to rest. Nina Ivanovna played on the piano for a bit, and then she too went away.

"Oh, dear Nadya!" Sasha said, starting up his usual afternoon conversation, "if only you would listen to me! If only!"

She was sitting deep in an old-fashioned armchair, her eyes shut, while he paced the room slowly from corner to corner.

"If only you would go to the university," he said. "Only enlightened and holy people are interesting, it's only they who are needed. The more of such people there are, the sooner the Kingdom of God will arrive on earth. Of your town then not one stone will be left, everything will he torn from its foundations, everything will be changed as though by magic. And then there will be immense, magnificent houses here, wonderful gardens, marvelous fountains, remarkable people... But that's not what matters most. What matters most is that the crowd, in our sense of the word, in the sense in which it exists now – for it evil will cease to exist, because every man will believe and every man will know what he is living for and no one will seek moral support in the crowd. Dear Nadya, darling girl, go away! Show them all that you are sick of this stagnant, grey, sinful life. Prove it to yourself at least!"

"I can't, Sasha, I'm going to be married."

"Oh nonsense! Who needs that?"

They went out into the garden and walked up and down a little.

"And no matter what, my dear, you must think, you must realize how unclean, how immoral this idle life of yours is," Sasha continued. "Do understand that if, for instance, you and your mother and your Granny do nothing, it means that someone else is working for you, you are eating up someone else's life. Is that really pure, isn't it filthy?"

Nadya wanted to say "Yes, that is true"; she wanted to say that she understood, but her eyes filled with tears, she suddenly became very quiet, shrunk into herself she went off to her room.

Towards evening Andrey Andreyich arrived and as usual played the violin for a long time. As a rule, he was not very talkative and loved the violin, perhaps because one could be silent while playing. At eleven o'clock, as he was leaving for home and had put on his greatcoat, he embraced Nadya and began to greedily kiss her face, her shoulders, her hands.

"My dear, my sweet, my charmer," he muttered. "Oh how happy I am! I am beside myself with ecstasy!"

And it seemed to her as though she had heard this long, long ago, or had read it somewhere… in some tattered old novel long since thrown away.

In the dining-room Sasha was sitting at the table drinking tea, the saucer balanced on his five long fingers; Granny was laying out Solitaire; Nina Ivanovna was reading. The flame crackled in the icon lamp and all, it seemed, was quiet and comfortable. Nadya said goodnight, went upstairs to her room, got into bed and fell asleep at once. But just as on the night before, just before it became light, she woke up. She did not feel sleepy, and her soul was weighed down by an uneasy, oppressive feeling. She sat up with her head on her knees and thought of her fiancé and her marriage… She for some reason remembered that her mother had not loved her father and now had nothing and lived in complete dependence on her mother-in-law, Granny. And Nadya, no matter how long she thought about it, could not understand why she had previously seen something special and unusual in her mother, how it was she had not noticed that she was a simple, ordinary, unhappy woman.

And Sasha downstairs was not asleep, she could hear him coughing. He is a queer, naïve man, Nadya thought, and there seemed to be something absurd in his dreams, in all those marvellous gardens and wonderful fountains. But for some reason in his naïveté, and even in his absurdity, there was something so beautiful that as soon as she thought about the possibility of going to university, her entire heart and bosom were flooded with feelings of joy and rapture.

"But it is better not to think, better not to think . . ." she whispered. "I must not think of it."

"Tick-tock," tapped the watchman somewhere far away. "Tick-tock… tick-tock…"

III

In the middle of June Sasha suddenly became bored and made up his mind to return to Moscow.

"I can't live in this town," he said gloomily. "No running water, no sewers! It disgusts me to eat dinner here; the filth in the kitchen is incredible…"

"Wait a bit, prodigal son!" grandmother cajoled him, for some reason speaking in a whisper, "the wedding is on the seventh."

"I don't want to."

"But you meant to stay with us until September!"

"But now I don't want to. I must get to work."

The summer was grey and cold, the trees were wet, everything in the garden looked doleful and uninviting, which certainly did make one long to get to work. Unfamiliar women's voices were heard in the rooms both downstairs and upstairs, there was the rattle of a sewing machine in grandmother's room, they were working hard on the trousseau. Of fur coats alone, six were provided for Nadya, and the cheapest of them, in grandmother's words, had cost three hundred rubles! The fuss irritated Sasha; he stayed in his own room and was cross; but they convinced him to stay, and he promised not to leave before the first of July.

Time passed quickly. On St. Peter's Day5 after dinner, Andrey Andreyich took Nadya to Moscow Street to look once more at the house which had long since been rented and made ready for the young couple. It was a two-story house, but so far only the upper floor had been furnished. In the hall was a gleaming floor, parqueted and painted, Viennese chairs, a piano, a violin stand. There was the smell of paint. On the wall hung a large oil painting in a gold frame – a naked lady and beside her a purple vase with a broken handle.

"An exquisite picture," said Andrey Andreyich, sighing out of respect. "It's the work of the artist Shishmachevsky."6

Then there was the drawing-room with the round table, and a sofa and easy chairs upholstered in bright blue. Above the sofa was a large photograph of Father Andrey wearing a priest's velvet cap and decorations. Then they went into the dining-room in which there was a sideboard; then into the bedroom; here in the half dusk stood two beds side by side, and it looked as though the bedroom had been decorated with the idea that it would always be very pleasant there and could not possibly be anything else. Andrey Andreyich led Nadya about the rooms, all the while keeping his arm round her waist; and she felt weak and guilty. She hated all the rooms, the beds, the easy chairs; she was nauseated by the naked lady. It was clear to her now that she had stopped loving Andrey Andreyich or perhaps had never loved him at all; but how to say this and to whom to say it and with what object she did not understand, and could not understand, though she thought about it day and night... He held her round the waist, talked so affectionately, so modestly, was so happy, walking about this, his lodgings; yet she saw nothing in all this but vulgarity – stupid, naïve, unbearable vulgarity, and his arm round her waist felt as hard and cold as an iron hoop. And with each passing moment she was ready to run away, burst into sobs, throw herself out a window. Andrey Andreyich led her into the bathroom and here he touched a tap fixed in the wall and at once water flowed.

"What do you say to that?" he said, and laughed. "I had a 100 *vedro* tank7 put in the attic, and so now we shall have water."

They walked across the yard, then went into the street and took a cab. Thick dust clouds blew about, and it seemed as if was about to rain.

"You are not cold?" said Andrey Andreyich, screwing up his eyes at the dust.

She did not answer.

"Yesterday, you remember, Sasha blamed me for doing nothing," he said, after a brief silence. "Well, he is right, absolutely right! I do nothing and can do nothing. My dear, why is that? Why is it that the very thought that I may some day fix a cockade on my cap and go into the government service is so hateful to me? Why do I feel so uneasy when I see a lawyer or a Latin master or a member of the Zemstvo? O Mother Russia! O Mother Russia! How much longer can you bear the burden of so many idle and useless people! How many like me you support, long-suffering Mother!"

And from the fact that he did nothing he drew generalizations, seeing in it a sign of the times.

"When we are married let us go together into the country, my dear; there we will work! We will buy ourselves a little piece of land with a garden and a river, we will labor and watch life. Oh, how splendid that will be!"

He took off his hat, and his hair floated in the wind, while she listened to him and thought: "Good God, I wish I were home!" When they were near the house they overtook Father Andrey.

"Ah, here's father coming," cried Andrey Andreyich, delighted, and he waved his hat. "I love my dad really," he said as he paid the cabman. "He's a splendid old fellow, a dear old fellow."

Nadya went into the house, angry and unwell, thinking that there would be visitors all evening, that she would have to entertain them, to smile, to listen to the fiddle, to listen to all sorts of nonsense, and to talk of nothing but the wedding. Grandmother, dignified, gorgeous in her silk dress, and haughty as she always seemed before visitors, sat near the samovar. Father Andrey came in with his sly smile.

"I have the pleasure and blessed consolation of seeing you in good health," he said to grandmother, and it was hard to tell whether he was joking or speaking seriously.

IV

The wind was beating on the window and on the roof; there was a whistling sound, and in the stove the house spirit8 was plaintively and sullenly droning his song. It was past midnight; everyone in the house had gone to bed, but no one was asleep, and Nadya kept sensing that downstairs someone was playing the violin. There was a sharp bang; a shutter must have been torn off. A minute later, Nina Ivanovna came in in her nightgown, with a candle.

"What was that bang, Nadya?" she asked.

On that stormy night, her mother, with her hair in a single plait and a timid smile on her face, looked older, less beautiful and smaller. Nadya remembered how not long ago she had considered her mother an exceptional woman and had listened with pride to whatever words she said; and now she was completely unable to remember those words, everything that she recalled was so feeble and useless.

From the stove came the sound of several bass voices in chorus, and she even heard "O-o-o my G-o-od!" Nadya sat on her bed, and suddenly she clutched at her hair and burst into sobs.

"Mother, mother, my mother," she said. "If only you knew what is happening to me! I beg you, I beseech you, let me go away! I beseech you!"

"Where?" asked Nina Ivanovna, not understanding, and she sat down on the bed. "Go where?"

For a long while Nadya cried and could not utter a word.

"Let me leave the town," she said at last. "There must not and will not be a wedding, understand that! I don't love that man... I can't even speak about him."

"No, my child, no!" Nina Ivanovna said quickly, terribly alarmed. "Calm yourself – it's just because you are in low spirits. It will pass. This often happens. Most likely you have had a tiff with Andrey; but lovers' quarrels always end in kisses!"

"Oh, go away, mother, oh, go away," sobbed Nadya.

"Yes," said Nina Ivanovna after a pause, "not so long ago you were a baby, a little girl, and now you are betrothed. In nature there is a continual transmutation of substances. Before you know it, you will be a mother yourself and even an old woman, and you will have as rebellious a daughter as I have."

"My dear, sweet mother," said Nadya, "you are so clever, yet so unhappy. You are so very unhappy; why do you say such banal things? For God's sake, why?"

Nina Ivanovna wanted to say something, but could not utter a word; she gave a sob and went away to her room. The bass voices began droning in the stove again, and Nadya suddenly was frightened. She jumped out of bed and quickly went to her mother. Nina Ivanovna, her face tear-stained, lie in bed, wrapped in a pale blue quilt and holding a book in her hands.

"Mother, listen to me!" said Nadya. "I implore you to stop and consider! If you could only understand how petty and degrading our life is. My eyes have been opened, and I see it all now. And what is your Andrey Andreyich? Why, he is not intelligent, mother! Merciful heavens, do understand, mother, he is stupid!"

Nina Ivanovna abruptly sat up.

"You and your grandmother torment me," she said with a sob. "I want to live! to live," she repeated, and twice she beat her little fist upon her bosom. "Give me my freedom! I am still young, I want to live, and you two have made me into an old woman!"

She broke into bitter tears, lay down and curled up under the quilt, and looked so small, so pitiful, so foolish. Nadya went to her room, dressed, and sat at the window, waiting for the morning. She sat all night thinking, while someone seemed to be tapping on the shutters and whistling in the yard.

In the morning grandmother complained that the wind had blown down all the apples in the garden and toppled an old plum tree. It was grey, murky, cheerless, dark enough for candles; everyone complained of the cold, and the rain lashed the windows. After tea Nadya went into Sasha's room and without saying a word knelt down before an armchair in the corner and hid her face in her hands.

"What is it?" Sasha asked.

"I can't . . ." she said. "How I could go on living here before, I can't understand, I can't grasp! I despise my fiancé, I despise myself, I despise all this idle, pointless existence."

"Well, well," said Sasha, not yet grasping what was up. "That's all right… that's good."

"I am sick of this life," Nadya continued. "I can't endure another day here. Tomorrow I am leaving here. Take me with you for God's sake!"

For a minute Sasha looked at her in astonishment; at last he understood and was delighted as a child. He waved his arms and began pattering with his slippers as though he were dancing with delight.

"Splendid," he said, rubbing his hands. "My goodness, how fine that is!"

And she stared at him unblinking, with big, adoring eyes, as though spellbound, expecting with each passing moment that he would say something important, something infinitely significant; he had told her nothing yet, yet already it seemed to her as if something new and great was opening before her, something previously unknown to her, and she gazed at him full of expectation, ready to face anything, even death.

"I am leaving tomorrow," he said after a moment's thought. "You come to the station to see me off... I'll take your things in my portmanteau, and I'll get your ticket, and when the third bell rings you get into the carriage, and we'll go off. You'll see me as far as Moscow and then go on to Petersburg alone. Have you a passport?"9

"Yes."

"I can promise you, you won't regret it," Sasha said with conviction. "You will go, you will study, and then go where fate takes you. When you turn your life upside down, everything will change. The main thing is to turn your life upside down, and all the rest is unimportant. And so we will set off tomorrow?"

"Oh yes, for God's sake!"

It seemed to Nadya that she was extremely agitated, that her soul was heavier than ever before, that until she departed she would have to suffer and be tormented by her thoughts; but hardly had she gone upstairs and lain down on her bed when she immediately fell sound asleep, with traces of tears and a smile on her face, until evening.

V

A cab had been sent for. Nadya, in her hat and overcoat, went upstairs to take one more look at her mother, at all her belongings. She stood in her own room beside her still warm bed, looked about her, then went slowly in to her mother. Nina Ivanovna was asleep; it was quite still in her room. Nadya kissed her mother, smoothed her hair, stood still for a couple of minutes... Then she returned unhurriedly downstairs.

It was raining heavily. The covered cab stood at the entrance, drenched with rain.

"There's no room for you, Nadya," grandmother said as the servants began loading the luggage. "What an idea to see him off in such weather! You would be better off staying home. Goodness, how it rains!"

Nadya tried to say something, but could not. Then Sasha helped Nadya in and covered her feet with a rug. Then he sat down beside her.

"Good luck to you! God bless you!" grandmother cried from the steps. "Mind you, write to us from Moscow, Sasha!"

"Right. Goodbye, Granny."

"The Queen of Heaven keep you!"

"Oh, what weather!" said Sasha.

It was only now that Nadya began to cry. It was now clear to her that she was definitely going, something she had not really believed when she was saying goodbye to grandmother, and when she was looking at her mother. Goodbye, town! And she suddenly thought of it all: Andrey, his father, the new house and the naked lady with the vase; all of it no longer frightened her, nor weighed upon her, but was naïve and trivial and was now retreating further behind her. And when they sat in the railcar and the train began to move, all of the former things which had been so great and serious shrank to a tiny lump, and before her unfolded a vast, wide future – one which had before been scarcely noticeable. The rain pattered on the carriage windows, nothing could be seen but green fields; there was the flash of telegraph posts and birds sitting on the wires, and joy suddenly made her catch her breath; she remembered that she was going toward her freedom, going to study, and this was just like what used, ages ago, to be called going off to be a free Cossack.10 She laughed and cried and prayed all at once.

"It's a-all right," said Sasha, smiling. "It's a-all right."

VI

Autumn had passed and winter followed close behind. Nadya had begun to be very homesick and thought every day of her mother and her grandmother; she thought of Sasha too. The letters that came from home were kind and gentle, and it seemed as though everything by now was forgiven and forgotten. In May, after exams, she set off for home in good health and high spirits, and stopped on the way in

Moscow to see Sasha. He was just the same as the year before, with the same beard and unkempt hair, with the same large, beautiful eyes, and he still wore the same coat and canvas trousers; but he looked unwell and worried, he seemed both older and thinner, and kept coughing, and for some reason he struck Nadya as grey and provincial.

"My God, Nadya has come!" he said, and laughed gaily. "My dear one!"

They sat in the printing room, which was full of tobacco smoke, and smelt strongly, stiflingly of inks; then they went to his room, which also smelt of tobacco and was full of the traces of spit; near a cold samovar stood a broken plate with dark paper on it, and there were masses of dead flies on the table and on the floor. And in everything it was evident that Sasha ordered his personal life in a slovenly way and lived as he wanted, with utter contempt for comfort, and if anyone began talking to him of his personal happiness, of his personal life, of affection for him, he would not have understood and would have only laughed.

"It's all right, everything has gone well," said Nadya hurriedly. "Mother came to see me in Petersburg in the autumn; she said that grandmother is not angry, and just keeps going into my room and making the sign of the cross to the walls."

Sasha looked cheerful, but he kept coughing, and talked in a cracked voice, and Nadya continued looking at him, unable to decide whether he really were seriously ill or whether it was just her interpretation of things.

"Dear Sasha," she said, "you are ill."

"No, it's nothing, I am ill, but not very . . ."

"Oh, dear!" cried Nadya, in agitation. "Why don't you go to a doctor? Why don't you take care of your health? My dear, darling Sasha," she said, and tears gushed from her eyes and for some reason there rose before her imagination Andrey Andreyich and the naked lady with the vase, and all her past which seemed now as distant as her childhood; and she began crying because Sasha no longer seemed to her so novel, so cultured, and so interesting as he did last year. "Dear Sasha, you are very, very ill… I would do anything to make you not so pale and thin. I am so indebted to you! You can't imagine how much you have done for me, my good Sasha! In reality you are now the person nearest and dearest to me."

They sat and talked, and now that Nadya had spent a winter in Petersburg, Sasha – his words, his smile, his whole figure – had for her a suggestion of something out of date, old-fashioned, done with long ago and perhaps already dead and buried.

"I am going down the Volga the day after tomorrow," said Sasha, "and then to drink *koumiss*. I want to drink *koumiss*.11 A friend and his wife are going with me. His wife is a wonderful woman; I am always at her, trying to persuade her to go to the university. I want her to turn her life upside down."

After they finished talking, they drove to the station. Sasha treated her to tea and apples; and when the train began moving and he waved his handkerchief at her, smiling, it was apparent even in his legs that he was very ill and would not live long.

Nadya reached her hometown at midday. As she drove home from the station, the streets struck her as very wide and the houses very small and squat; there were no people about, she met no one but the German piano-tuner in a rusty greatcoat. All the houses were covered with dust. Grandmother, who seemed to have grown quite old, but was as fat and plain as ever, flung her arms round Nadya and cried for a long time with her face on Nadya's shoulder, unable to tear herself away. Nina Ivanovna looked much older and plainer and seemed shrivelled up, but was still tightly laced, and still had diamonds flashing on her fingers.

"My darling," she said, trembling all over, "my darling!"

Then they sat down and cried without speaking. It was clear that both mother and grandmother realized that the past was lost for good, never to return; they had now no position in society, no prestige as before, no right to invite visitors; it is the same as when, in the midst of an easy, careless life, the police suddenly burst in at night and make a search, and it turns out that the head of the house has embezzled money or committed forgery – goodbye then to the easy, careless life for ever!

Nadya went upstairs and saw the same bed, the same windows with naïve white curtains, and outside the windows the same garden, gay and noisy, bathed in sunshine. She touched her table, sat down and sank into thought. And she had a good dinner and drank tea with delicious rich cream; but something was missing, there was a sense of emptiness in the rooms and the ceilings were so low. In the evening she went to bed, covered herself up and for some reason it seemed humorous to her to be lying in this warm, very soft bed.

Nina Ivanovna came in for a minute; she sat as guilty people do, timidly, glancing about.

"Well, tell me, Nadya," she asked after a brief pause, "are you content? Quite content?"

"Yes, mother."

Nina Ivanovna got up, made the sign of the cross over Nadya and the windows.

"I have become religious, as you see," she said. "You know I am studying philosophy now, and I am always thinking and thinking... And many things have become as clear as day. It seems to me that what is above all necessary is that life should pass as it were through a prism."

"Tell me, mother, how is grandmother's health?"

"She seems all right. When you went away back then with Sasha and when the telegram came from you, grandmother fell on the floor as she read it; for three days she lay without moving. After that she was constantly praying and crying. But now she is fine."

She got up and walked about the room.

"Tick-tock," tapped the watchman. "Tick-tock, tick-tock. . . ."

"What is above all necessary is that life should pass as it were through a prism," she said; "in other words, that life in consciousness should be divided into its simplest elements as if into the seven primary colors, and each element must be studied separately."

What Nina Ivanovna said further and when she went away, Nadya did not hear, as she quickly fell asleep.

May passed; June came. Nadya had grown used to being at home. Grandmother busied herself about the samovar, sighing deeply. Nina Ivanovna talked in the evenings about her philosophy; she still lived in the house like a poor relation, and had to go to grandmother for every littlest bit of cash. There were lots of flies in the house, and the ceilings seemed to be getting lower and lower. Granny and Nina Ivanovna did not go outside for fear of meeting Father Andrey and Andrey Andreyich. Nadya walked about the garden and the streets, looked at the grey fences, and it seemed to her that everything in the town had long since grown old, was out of date and was just waiting either for the end, or for the beginning of something young, something fresh. Oh, if only that new, bright life would come more quickly – that life where one can look boldly and directly at one's fate, to know that one is right, to be light-hearted and free! And sooner or later such a life will come! The time will come when, at grandmother's house – where things are so arranged that the four servants must live in one filthy basement room – the time will come when not a trace will remain of that house; it will be forgotten, no one will remember it. And Nadya's only entertainment was from the boys next door; when she walked about the garden they knocked on the fence and shouted in mockery: "Bride! Bride!"

A letter from Sasha arrived from Saratov. In his gay, dancing handwriting he told them that his journey on the Volga had been a complete success, but that he had been taken rather ill in Saratov, had lost his voice, and had been for the last fortnight in the hospital. She knew what that meant, and she was overwhelmed with a foreboding that was like a conviction. And it vexed her that this foreboding and the thought of Sasha did not distress her so much as before. She had a passionate desire for life, longed to be in Petersburg, and her friendship with Sasha seemed now sweet but something far, far away! She did not sleep all night, and in the morning sat at the window, listening. And she did in fact hear voices below; grandmother, greatly agitated, was rapidly asking questions about something. Then someone began crying... When Nadya went downstairs, grandmother was standing in the corner, praying before the icon, her face covered with tears. A telegram lay on the table.

For some time Nadya walked up and down the room, listening to grandmother's weeping; then she picked up the telegram and read it. It announced that the previous morning Alexander Timofeyich, or more simply, Sasha, had died of consumption in Saratov.

Grandmother and Nina Ivanovna went to the church to order a memorial service, while Nadya went on walking about the rooms and thinking. She recognized clearly that her life had been turned upside down as Sasha wished; that here she was alone, alien, useless, and that everything here was useless to her, that all that had come before had been ripped from her and had vanished as though it had been burnt up and the ashes scattered to the winds. She went into Sasha's room and stood there for a while.

"Goodbye, dear Sasha," she thought, and before her mind arose the vision of a new, wide, spacious life, and that life, still obscure and full of mysteries, beckoned and attracted her.

She went upstairs to her room to pack, and the next morning she said goodbye to her family and, full of life and high spirits, left the town – for good, she presumed.

1903

ABOUT THE AUTHOR

Anton Pavlovich Chekhov (1860-1904) is widely considered one of history's finest writers of short stories and plays. Indeed, it could well be argued that he invented or at least perfected the short story.

Born the child of a shopkeeper who had earned his way out of serfhood (slavery), Chekhov trained to be a doctor, which eventually allowed him to support his family, but his true passion was for storytelling. "Medicine is my lawful wife," he once said, "and literature is my mistress."

As a writer and storyteller, Chekhov was astoundingly prolific (over 500 stories in his short life) and repeatedly profound. He had a gift for recounting passionate, moving, powerful moments of human existence in a style that was eloquent yet understated. "You may weep and moan over your stories," he once advised a young writer, "you may suffer with your heroes, but I consider that one must do this so that the reader does not notice it. The more objective, the stronger will be the effect."

There are several fine biographies of Chekhov that do the man far more justice than this cursory aside. *Chekhov: A Life*, by Donald Rayfield, is highly recommended. And a brand new account of Chekhov's literary turning point, *Chekhov Becomes Chekhov*, by Robert Blaisdell, is also highly recommended.